"A funny, ironic work about a serious business, the monolithic, perhaps dangerously archaic machinery of the State Department and the labyrinthine processes of diplomacy . . . witty, earthy, and absorbing."
— *San Francisco Chronicle*

"What sets this novel apart from the fat cats we have had about our national capital is Galbraith's irreverence, his cool wit, and his perception of policy making which only an insider could gibe at so effectually."
— *The Atlantic Monthly*

"Galbraith has turned his talents to fiction and produced a novel which a great many readers will consume with amusement and no doubt a measure of enlightenment . . . Hardly a paragraph goes by without some specimen of the Galbraith wit . . . The fun spreads over a wide range."
— *Boston Globe*

Novels by John Kenneth Galbraith

THE MCLANDRESS DIMENSION
A TENURED PROFESSOR
THE TRIUMPH

·

John Kenneth Galbraith

THE TRIUMPH

A Novel of Modern Diplomacy

WITH A NEW INTRODUCTION
BY THE AUTHOR

Houghton Mifflin Company

BOSTON NEW YORK

For information about permission
to reproduce selections from this book,
write to Permissions, Houghton Mifflin Company,
215 Park Avenue South, New York, New York 10003.

Library of Congress Cataloguing-in-Publication Data
Galbraith, John Kenneth, date.
The triumph : a novel of modern diplomacy /
John Kenneth Galbraith
p.   cm.
ISBN 0-395-66513-2
1. Diplomats — United States — Fiction.
2. Diplomats — Latin America — Fiction.   I. Title.
PS3557.A4113T7 1993   93-18169
813'.54—dc20   CIP

Printed in the United States of America

BP 10 9 8 7 6 5 4 3 2 1

For Averell Harriman

On Writing
Ahead of the Times

Introduction to the 1993 Edition
JOHN KENNETH GALBRAITH

WHILE ALL SUCH SUGGESTIONS must be viewed with deep skepticism, this book, which first came out in 1968, a quarter of a century ago, can reasonably be said to have been ahead of its time. It was not for that reason neglected; it was for rewarding weeks on the best-seller lists. It also had an excellent claim on attention in numerous other countries, including most spectacularly perhaps, Brazil, where my politically well motivated publisher Carlos Lacerda advertised it like cigarettes on billboards leading into Rio and São Paulo, after which the seriously perverse government of the time suppressed it. On a trip I made to Brazil years later, people proudly brought brown, acid-ridden copies from their shelves for me to autograph.

It was also sold two or three times to the movies, once with a script that I had been commissioned to write. In keeping with Hollywood tradition, it was bought and paid for but not produced. It did appear as a play not too distant from Broadway; mercifully, it closed after a few florid exhibitions. I am not good at love scenes; those in an early draft of the novel were said by Arthur Schlesinger, Jr., to read like something done for research purposes at the Boston Lying In Hospital. I took them out. In consequence,

Clare Boothe Luce, when reviewing it, said it could be "the only attempt made in the past decade to write a novel that is totally devoid of any love or sex interest." In the play my omission was corrected; the players were put into bed at predictably short intervals, sometimes, as I recall, without shaking hands. So far as I know, there was no ensuing pregnancy or abortion. That, theatrically speaking, would have been the only interesting effect.

The much better success of the book as a book derived from its more solemn purpose. That was to see and, in a sensitive way, to deride the then-current preoccupation with Communism in the Americas, as also in the other poor countries of the globe. This concern was central at the time and for many years in sophisticated, articulate, and assertive foreign-policy thought or what is so denoted. It was also profoundly, if pridefully, insane. Now, many years, many billions of dollars, and many young lives later, we largely accept that this was the case.

Then scholars and officials proved their professionalism by their evident alertness to a worldwide Communist menace. They were members of a club in which all embraced the common truth. They showed their adaptability of mind by accepting and sophisticating the conservative anti-Communist paranoia. Some rejoiced in the hard-nosed masculinity that made them willing, often eager supporters of the promiscuous use of military force. No general would ever emerge from the Pentagon and say that *they* were soft on Communism in Vietnam or a dozen other unfortunate lands. Their penalty for this aberration has not been slight: they cannot now read the voluminous histories of this period without finding themselves criticized, pilloried, even disdained. The more paranoid conservatives and the military leaders are more fortunate; they almost certainly do not read these books.

The remarkable thing about this foreign-policy community was that, with rare exceptions, its members were serious, well-educated citizens with a strong commitment to the public service and the public purpose. Not all, to be sure: the more dubious of the covert operations had for long attracted a small convocation of accomplished rascals. In later times some even more questionable felons emerged to collect and appropriate cash. (The war in Nicaragua and the Iran-Contra operation were especially so milked.) But in the White House, the State Department, the military establishment, and elsewhere, the participants, both professional and political, were mostly in pursuit of what they saw as the public good.

My own, and different view on this matter must be attributed rather more to fortunate experience than to superior insight. I had been much in Asia, particularly when I was Ambassador to India. President Kennedy had sent me briefly to Vietnam. I had also been fairly often in Latin America, a part of the world I had learned to love. And I had come to the conclusion, by no means original, that Communism — comprehensive socialism — was not possible before there was capitalism. Riding out from Saigon one day, I was struck by the difficulty in telling a Communist jungle from a capitalist jungle. There was a similar problem in persuading poor, self-sufficient villagers as to that difference when they had not experienced either system.

Indian villagers, I had come to know, were also uninformed by any experience as to the difference, but they did know about foreign rule. That was part of their history going back a thousand years. Some had even heard that Americans might be the latest intruders. It was wholly plausible that we would be so regarded in Vietnam. There we would be identified with French colonial rule, for many with whom we were allied had been so associated. In Latin America, and particularly in Central America, the United States, the colossus to the north, was also far more visible and to many more relevant than the distant world of the late Marx, Lenin, and Joseph Vissarionovich Stalin.

In the 1960s, these views had a marginal, even fugitive existence in Washington. President Kennedy was not unreceptive; his taste for a deeper Vietnam involvement was well under control. Arthur Schlesinger, Jr., Richard Goodwin, and later Bill Moyers, all with presidential access, were opposed to it or in doubt. So in the State Department in the earliest days of the new administration was Chester Bowles, the Under Secretary, as, with later influence, was George Ball. (Bowles was soon excised for his heresy.)

Standing against were the foreign-policy scholars, the massive force of the State Department bureaucracy and culture, the Secretary of State himself, and, needless perhaps to say, the military establishment. Communism was on the march; the dominoes would fall. Do not listen to Galbraith: he is not useful.

After some time I decided to go public. Nothing so serves the ego as being on the inside when great decisions are involved. Nothing is quite so humbling as being neither within nor without, which was my case. So I began speaking against our preoccupation with Communism in what was now being called the Third World and especially in Vietnam. In an exercise in democratic centralism that would have impressed Lenin, the late Joseph Rauh arranged that I be made Chairman of Americans for Democratic Action, the organization that was then the acknowledged voice of liberalism. It was a needed political platform. I then helped persuade Eugene McCarthy to take up the cause against Vietnam and was, in a manner of speaking, his floor manager at the great and wildly uninhibited convention in Chicago in 1968. I seconded his nomination in a sterling address to which no one in that vast hall paid the slightest attention, at least until I attacked my fellow public statesman John Connally of Texas, the leader of the opposition forces.

Gene had been condemned by an earlier speaker as a poet. I, as I've often told, responded: "My friends, this may not be the age of John Milton, but *it is not* the age of John Wayne or John Connally." Suddenly previously somnambulant partisans rose from their seats to shove their state banners down and up in the air and shout, "Fuck Connally." John was very nice. In reply, he was quoted as saying, "Down in Texas where Ah come from, it heps to have that Galbraith agin ya."

.

Meanwhile I had written a novel to advance the cause. I wanted to show, above all, the cultivated, highly formalized obliquity with which foreign-policy decisions were made, particularly those concerning Communism in the industrially undeveloped lands, where it was deeply irrelevant.

It was not the first time I sought to convey truth in fiction. While in the foreign-policy establishment as Ambassador, I had written a collection of fictional pieces under the pseudonym of Mark Epernay. The book told, along with much else, of how the State Department had designed early computer software that allowed an automatic response to all foreign-policy developments, thus dispensing with any and all personnel, the Secretary of State himself excepted. "We are watching closely the situation in Pago Pago. If any threat to the free world develops there, we are fully ready to take the appropriate action." Or language to that effect. With foresight I would have said Grenada.

.

It will be asked, and rightly, why wanting to deal with this highly developed mental aberration, I did not center the novel on Vietnam. That unhappy country was closest to my thoughts, for it was there that the greatest tragedy was being played out. Why the less poignant error in Central America?

To this day I am not completely certain as to the wisdom of my decision. Then, however, the basic reason seemed clear: I wanted to deal in ridicule — ridicule that solemnly and persuasively depicted the gravely deranged. That was the weapon I had at hand. But Vietnam was too tragic for this instrument. Too many were too deeply, too cruelly, engaged. Too many were dying. One could condemn in speech; to the best of my ability that is what I did. But one could not seem to be having fun while doing so. Latin America, especially the small states of Central America, served better my case against the compulsive cold warriors as they operated in the poor lands. There ridicule would work.

And there subsequent events were to justify my case. For long years in El Salvador and then with high visibility in Nicaragua, including the enduring Iran-Contra episode, the threat of Latin American Communism deeply affected the more available and, alas, the more influential foreign-policy minds. Now, in retrospect, that preoccupation does seem foolish. I sought to depict it so at the time.

·

I do not want to suggest that I approached this book with a total solemnity of purpose. I wrote part of it in Switzerland, where for thirty years and more years I've retreated from reality to writing. Some of it I wrote in Venice, which is why buildings in Flores have Italian facades. (Early on I explained that, to design this unfortunate capital, a misplaced Venetian architect had been employed.) Some of it I wrote in Majorca, when I persuaded myself that I needed to be closer to a Spanish scene. And some I wrote with no similarly questionable justification amidst the maples of Vermont. Without exaggeration I can say I enjoyed every moment of my task. For one thing, all of my characters in this book are based on real people. All were once in office. I merely mixed up their speech, appearance, and official positions so that no one was seriously recognizable.

It has often been said by writers seeking social purpose for their toil that one can come closer to reality in fiction than in decently confirmed fact. One can adjust the world so as to show the reality. I believe this to be so; there is even more pleasure, a certain feeling of legitimate meanness, in dealing with the characters one assembles out of reality. In light of previous dismissal, one is settling those old scores, getting even.

I wrote this novel when I was turning sixty. Perhaps it is well that it came so late in life. Had I experienced the pleasures of fiction earlier, I might have done nothing else. That, remaining as I did at Harvard, would have strained the tolerance we are so justly allowed in academic life.

•

This, as I have said, is a treatise on public error — error by well-intentioned persons submitting to collective stupidity. It is something we will not escape in the future, for it is also, we should note, a feature of great organization, and it is great and complex organization that characterizes the modern state. Such organization, civilian or military, public or private, comes to have a commonly accepted policy: this is State Department policy; this is Air Force doctrine; this is how we must see the war on drugs. It is usually a measure of one's worth that one seeks to change wrong policy; sadly, within the organization, it is a measure of worth that one accepts the established policy.

So, in some measure, it must be. The policy is what unites diverse talents and specialties in common action. I have not been easy in this book on those who were so united in the fear of Communism in the Third World. But many were the captives of the organization of which they were a part. So even, in marked measure, are Presidents. I write here about a mildly skeptical President — my mind, needless to say, went back to John F. Kennedy. But, on matters affecting the small land of Puerto Santos, he was sadly subordinate to the organization that nominally he headed.

As I write this, we are in the midst of the quadrennial carnival that is commonly referred to as an election campaign. It is deemed an event of overwhelming importance. Political savants with their passion for the commonplace are noting that the individual soon to be elected will be the most powerful figure in what, until lately, was called the free world.

The American Presidency is not an unimportant post. Nor is that of President, Chancellor, Prime Minister, Chief Minister, or whatever the designation in other lands. We make a serious mistake, however, if we do not see that in the modern polity this is also a sharply circumscribed authority. There is the normal and accepted constraint of the Congress, Parliament, or other elected body. There is the subtle and far-less-publicized constraint of organization and the accepted view. This will be true of Presidents of whatever political faith or party in the United States as they deal with the State Department, the Central Intelligence Agency, and, notably, with the commanding authority of the Pentagon. All these have their conforming policy; some of it will be as irrelevant as the threat of Communism from Grenada — or Puerto Santos. The glowing errors of policy as opposed to intelligence in an age of great organization, sometimes called bureaucracy, are a fact of life. They are also a central message of this book.

This message contended, however, with a certain elusive hope. It was that in pursuing solemn purpose, I would not deny the reader a goodly measure of valid enjoyment, even fun. I again affirm that hope.

Explanation . . .

THIS IS A STORY I have tried to tell before in articles and lectures. But it has occurred to me that maybe there are truths that best emerge from fiction. I did hesitate to describe this small fable as a novel; there is, as the reader will discover, too much attempted instruction by the author. Perhaps Truman Capote would wish to call it a non-novel novel.

None of the characters in this book is imaginary; all have been assembled in bits and pieces from people I have known in public life. But the pieces were much too small for anyone to be recognized as a living person. I say this for it would be a waste of time for anyone to go fishing here for his friends, his enemies or even himself. Nor would I wish it thought that I was using a fable to say things I would not otherwise put in print. As some will be aware, I have not, in recent years, been wholly reticent as a critic of our foreign policy.

J.K.G.

1

IN WHAT IS STILL CALLED the New State Department Building in Washington, the offices of the highest officials are on the seventh floor. And the very highest officials — the Secretary and the two Under Secretaries who are concerned with diplomacy as distinct from the man who posts people to jobs, prepares the budget and insures the security of communications — are in a small enclave with its own small corridor, access to which is protected by a receptionist who stops all visitors and politely inquires as to their business, making an exception only of a few favored officials whom she knows. These, from her desk in the large foyer, she greets by name or title — Mr. Nitze, Mr. Helms, Mr. Ambassador — as they stride by and disappear along the small corridor just mentioned.

The building was completed during the secretaryship of Mr. John Foster Dulles, and much of his personality and more of his policy are reflected in this suite of offices. The offices themselves are vast and paneled in dark mahogany, and there is so much of it as, somewhat unfortunately, to suggest a rather thin veneer of plywood, and the eye searches unconsciously for cracks. The furniture is heavy and the leather very brown and official. In addition to the receptionist the entrance to the suite is guarded by two giant blocks of white marble. Each must weigh several tons. Nearby, somewhat irrelevantly, is a handsome grandfather's clock. Lining the walls of the small corridor are oil portraits of past Secretaries of State. Until the time of William Jennings Bryan these have a certain dignity; thereafter they deteriorate rapidly in quality and style, and that of James F. Byrnes slightly suggests a fugitive from justice and Edward R. Stettinius, one who has just been apprehended. Dean Acheson looks spiritual and surprised. The general effect, not alone of the portraits, is hideous and admirably reflects Mr. Dulles's conviction that diplomacy pays no homage to lesser art. Nothing need serve the purposes of grace or decoration; everything should be to impress or possibly to intimidate. Elsewhere in the building, where these effects are not required, the aspect is very different — rather that of an unusually well-staffed hospital.

An exception is a small room on the eighth floor — a floor used not for offices but for official receptions, state luncheons and dinners and other occasions of high protocol. Here also is the executive dining room. It is of modest size, simply furnished and rather cheerful — there are small tables for two along the walls and larger ones toward the middle. From the ample windows one can see the Potomac and the Pentagon. The food, like the furniture, is functional. No alcohol, not even beer, is served, and diplomats back from abroad for consultation find it a relief from the cocktails, canapés, the succession of courses, and wines, and the coffee and brandy without which, at any meal in line of duty, the dignity of a great nation would not be upheld.

•

The very highest officials of the Department do not eat their lunch in the pleasant room on the top floor, and this poses a small problem for the officials just below. The Secretary, the Under Secretary and any Assistant Secretary who has a serious problem on his hands are much too busy for the leisurely and congenial ways of a restaurant. Lunch is a time for an intense tête-à-tête with some other official, a *tour d'horizon* with a visiting foreign minister, for conveying, as they are called, the hard facts of life to the ambassador of some friendly but, as seen by the State Department, politically retarded nation, or for catching up with urgent memoranda and telegrams. All are best accomplished over a tray in one's own office. Or these men are commanded to the White House for obeisance to a visiting potentate or to a foreign embassy for the same purpose, from which they return feeling a trifle hazy and overfed. The most senior officials being so occupied, a slightly lesser man loses caste if his meal seems to be without urgency. So, quite often, he has a sandwich and some coffee brought to his office, and he consumes them all by himself while occupying himself with research reports and congressional testimony he does not need to read. This prudence is required especially of men of the rank of Assistant Secretary. As late as Roosevelt's time there were only two in the entire Department of State, and so great was their distinction that one of them, Raymond Moley, never ceased to believe that his views were entitled to rather greater respect than those of the President himself. Now the *Congressional Directory* lists no fewer than nine officers of this title, and as many more are thought to have the same rank and pay. This dilution has had its inevitable effect; those who hold the office sense the danger of their descending into the official proletariat. It is wise to take precautions.

And yet the dining room, apart from providing nourishment in a pleasant and calming atmosphere, serves an important public function. One can there acquire or offer information too speculative to be presented in the Secretary's morning staff meeting, or to be circulated as a piece of paper, or to appear in a telegram, or which hasn't been sufficiently certified so that it can go into the weekly intelligence summaries circulated by the CIA. And such information is vital, for what comes in these regular sources of information is what one already knows. A man who lunches alone does not pick up that first glimmering hint of great events ahead. Nor does he acquire a reputation as a man who foresees such events. Certainly if something important seems to be in the wind, he is wise to risk his reputation and go to the executive dining room.

Something — perhaps not much — was in the wind on the day this history begins. For nearly a fortnight, or more, there had been rumors of a revolution in Puerto

Santos. Now the papers told of actual fighting. Puerto de los Santos, to accord this nation its full grammatical dignity, is not an important country. But it is the peculiar, and perhaps the unique, genius of American diplomacy that it regularly brings great if somewhat temporary importance to highly unimportant lands. This it has done for Laos, the Dominican Republic, most notably for Vietnam, and for the Congo, Yemen, Thailand and Panama. All with a legitimate concern for Latin American affairs, and everyone with an interest in Central American and Caribbean questions, were more than a little on the alert.

"What's your assessment of our situation in P.S.?" The question came from a small, slight man with a long intelligent face, unkempt hair flecked with gray and a tweed jacket which, although at some sacrifice of elegance, concealed the dandruff. He put the question hurriedly before the menu had been quite circulated, for it was evident that he wanted to get the conversation on a firm professional track. Worth Campbell, to whom the question was addressed, looked reflectively at the small man for a moment or two.

No one doubted that he was the man to be questioned and to answer. Others might have opinions; Assistant Secretary of State for Inter American Affairs and U.S. Coordinator, Alliance for Progress, Dr. Grant Worthing Campbell had a position. When he did answer, his voice was nicely modulated, mellow, confident and attractive. It went well with his white hair, high forehead and smooth, pink, almost youthful complexion. Only his eyes, rather small and obviously a trifle infirm behind their rimless spectacles, were out of keeping. They had a schoolmasterish, some would say slightly querulous, quality.

"You make the country sound like an afterthought. Maybe it was meant to be. I'd say yes and no. Anyhow, that's a good diplomatic answer!"

"What I mean is, can the Obregón administration in your judgment survive?"

"Martínez, it is really." The voice was now almost deliberately gentle. "You scholars in Policy Planning must remember that while the Spaniards are nice to their mothers they use their father's name for everyday. You have seen the same telegrams I have. Pethwick believes Martínez has the strength to ride this one out. Over the longer run the picture isn't so clear. But then in the long run we are all dead. That was Keynes, wasn't it?"

The others at the table obviously approved the estimate, and several bowed in agreement. But the little man was not quite finished. "Our preliminary analyses in PP show that there are considerable grounds for dissatisfaction down there."

"There probably are. And you can never tell how much more is boiling just below the surface. But so far the old man has kept things pretty well under control. And, everything considered, he's been a good friend of ours. The Communists don't like him, and he's been willing to put up with quite a lot from some of our well-meaning people. I'd be the first to admit that some of his methods aren't entirely to our liking."

An AID man, the Assistant Administrator for Program,

Material Resources and Finance, had pulled his chair over from an adjacent table. The Assistant Secretary turned to him: "Remind us what we've got going down there now, John."

"The military program you know about. We have two pilot programs on land reform. We have just finished programming a new contract with Texas A. & M. for a college-of-agriculture project. There's a fishing project and related cold storage program. That's about all. The *campesinos* divided up our experimental farm when they tried to move onto the big estates in the high country in '60. Martínez decided to let them keep our property. He said it showed that he accepted a land reform program in principle."

"There's also the budget support?"

"Christ, yes! There is also the budget support! With the military, that is *the* program. Every time Pethwick has seen Martínez in the past two years it has cost us another $5 million. He keeps needing more and getting less — except from us."

"Well, it hasn't been a bad investment — so far." As the others again bowed in agreement a man across the table caught Worth Campbell's eye.

"Doctor, how would you appraise Puerto Santos from the standpoint of free world security?" The questioner was a slender good-looking man of about forty with short blond hair and a rugged, healthy face. In contrast with the man from Policy Planning, he wore a neat, almost natty, blue pinstripe. He looked extremely clean.

"That's really your department — Colonel Massey, isn't

it? I assume the Air Force has a pretty good view. We certainly don't want the Communists stepping over Rostow's truce line in that part of the world. It would give our comrade friends a new chance in Guatemala and Venezuela, maybe Colombia. We have to remember that not all the dominoes are in Asia. And there is always the Canal to think about."

"Would you say that there is an alternative to this President Martínez, Doctor?"

"There are always alternatives, Colonel — that's my experience in Latin America, anyhow. But they are not always better and sometimes a lot worse, and no one can tell which will be which. So you stand by what friends you have — or you should. I wish more of our people understood that simple law of life."

"Mr. Secretary, your secretary is on the line." It was the head waitress. Worth Campbell had a fleeting sense of relief. There was a question whether he should be here conducting a seminar at this particular time.

.

In his outer office, William (Bill) O'Donnell was waiting with the telegram.

"I estimate that this piece of shit will hit the fan upstairs in about one hour. I figured you might want a little head start."

The Assistant Secretary looked at O'Donnell with what he hoped was well-concealed repugnance. How he disliked the man. Irishmen and Catholics were comparatively rare in the Foreign Service. Once a monopoly of white Anglo-Saxon Protestants, it had become a comfortable coalition of these and socially concerned Jews. So it was possible that O'Donnell, in addition to all else, had to be forgiven for a form of minority assertiveness. But Worth Campbell preferred to believe that his manners compensated for a fairly mediocre career. O'Donnell was nearing forty and still a Class III officer. His present post, Acting Director of the Office of Central American and Caribbean Affairs, considering all of the strategic areas of American interest in the world, was pretty far down. In fact, O'Donnell did worry about this at times but not as much as might have been expected. Most aspects of his adult life had seemed an improvement over his early existence as one of the four sons of a Santa Fe section foreman from whose toiling minions he had learned his fluent and highly idiomatic Spanish. The O'Donnell children already showed signs of being more impatient.

In State Department usage the priority classification "Emergency" is one grade below that of "Critic" which is reserved for an outbreak of war or its equivalent. The telegram was as follows:

SECRET

Flores, P.S.

Emergency Limit Distribution

SEC STATE
WASHINGTON

HAVE JUST COMPLETED DETAILED URGENT COUNTRY TEAM REVIEW ALL ASPECTS LOCAL SITUATION. THOUGH SOME FEATURES UNCLEAR REMAIN CONFIDENT FUNDAMENTAL

STABILITY MARTINEZ REGIME AND CAPABILITY FOR CONTROLLING PRESENT INSURGENCY. HOWEVER THERE HAS BEEN FURTHER SERIOUS DETERIORATION LAST TWENTY-FOUR HOURS. SECURITY OF IMPORTANT AREAS OF FLORES INCLUDING JAIL, MUNICIPAL ABBATOIR, ESSO STORAGE TANKS NOW IN DOUBT ALTHOUGH GOVERNMENT ASSERTS INTENTION TAKING PROMPT STEPS TO RESTORE AUTHORITY. IN LAST TWO HOURS RADIO STATION HAS BEEN BROADCASTING SUBVERSIVE ANTI-MARTINEZ PROPAGANDA SUGGESTING POSSIBLE TAKE-OVER THIS FACILITY. HAVE APPOINTMENT MARTINEZ TONIGHT TWENTY-THREE HUNDRED HOURS FLORES TIME. FEEL THIS MUST BE OCCASION FOR DECISIVE ACTION PROMISING FULL U.S. MILITARY, ECONOMIC, MORAL SUPPORT FOR ALL-OUT COUNTER-INSURGENCY EFFORT. REQUEST URGENT REPLY SOONEST AUTHORIZING OFFER OF SUCH ASSISTANCE. IN ABSENCE CANNOT RULE OUT FURTHER DETERIORATION LEADING TO EARLY POSSIBLE TAKE-OVER BY UNFRIENDLY FORCES. STRESS AGAIN RESULTING GRAVE THREAT TO U.S. HEMISPHERE, FREE WORLD SECURITY IN THIS AREA OF VITAL AND STRATEGIC FREE WORLD INTEREST. REMAINING IN CLOSEST TOUCH ALL DEVELOPMENTS.

PETHWICK

The Assistant Secretary looked by O'Donnell to his secretary. "This is serious. Tell Symes — Mr. Jones — to come in. Phone the Secretary's office that I am standing by. They'll know why. I think maybe I better alert the White House."

2

IN THE ARCHIVO GENERAL DE INDIAS in Seville, that vast warehouse of the records of the Spanish colonial empire which proves that paper work is no latter-day passion of the bureaucrat, there is a plan of the city of Flores. It was submitted by an early governor, as was required of all, and it suggests more than a little of the pride of its creator. It is larger than the others, and it is in color. Streets, avenues, squares, *Gobernación, cuartel*, parade ground — the latter denoted by the grander French title of Champ de Mars — the Church of Our Lady of the Flowers and adjacent "palace" and the vast area reserved to the future occupancy of the cathedral and the university are all sketched in with a spacious hand. In the center of the present-day town traces of this intended grandeur are still to be seen.

Flores is on the tableland well above and away from the fetid coast and the Port of the Saints that named the country, and where, it was soon learned, not even the blessed could reliably survive. In the dry season, while it is hot in Flores in the daytime, it is much cooler at night, and visitors at this period agree that the climate, generally speaking, is delightful. Unfortunately there are six months of the year when not even the most predacious travel agent recommends a visit, for it rains for days at a time. The air is hot and moist and reminds the sensitive of the steam from a broken automobile radiator. The rains have eroded the buildings in the old city, and where they have been repaired, it has often been with different and cheaper material. The old facades are covered with a greenish mold; small thick-leaved plants have taken root in the crevices and grow around the wrought-iron porticoes. The effect is much more agreeable, however, than farther out the broad avenues where newer office buildings, square, barren and with too much glass, are streaked and stained by the rust from the metal sash, and where large steel and glass doors provide a glimpse of peeling paint, chipped floors, discarded beer bottles and ineffable shabbiness within. Yet farther out, beyond this domain of Philips, Shell, Bayer, Singer and the other heralds of the modern age, shabbiness gives way to squalor and squalor to poverty, abject, unapologetic and unrelieved.

Here the city pavement, pit-holed and often dangerous, but yet a decent alternative to the stinking mud, comes to an end. And instead of the nasty square buildings there are yet nastier huts. And instead of the rusty streaks on the concrete, there is a limitless expanse of rusty tin roofing. The best is not tin but rusty galvanized iron; from the remainder — beaten-out oil, beer, fruit, vegetable and condensed-milk cans — the thin coating of tin has long since disappeared. All is now a mottled, ragged, desolate brown. Children play in the mud by the roadside or are suckled by their mothers on the narrow veranda in front of each hut. Dogs and an occasional pig explore through the short stumps on which the better of these dwellings stand. There was once a convention that all garbage would be dumped in a drainage ditch that runs along the road and that all would repair to the ditch to defecate and pee. But this ordinance is ill-enforced, and in a Spanish culture, even among the poor, modesty has its claims. Between the houses are banana trees, and overtopping the houses is a thick fringe of palms. But unlike the trees in the more fortunate suburbs of more favored towns, their purpose is not alone to provide shade. It is also, alas, to contain the wet and preserve the mud and the noisome smells for the people who live among them. Meant to encircle all this is Paseo Roosevelt.

There are more pleasant regions. To the east, on a broad rise which begins a mile or two from the center of the old town, are the houses of the well-to-do and the foreigners. One street, favored by politicians, where in his better days President Martínez also went often to relax with a mistress, is referred to by the more circumspect guides as the street of the forty cabinet ministers, by bolder ones as that of the forty thieves. These houses stand in their own grounds behind low masonry walls. Here also are several Embassies, the Nuncio's residence and a luxury hotel with a fine kidney-shaped swimming pool. The hotel is in poor repair, and the swimming pool has not been used for a long while, for in recent years, even in the dry season, the tourist business has not been good. But this hill is a small island of opulence. Most of Flores is squalid.

·

At dawn there had been heavy small-arms fire in the north of the city. A secretary who lived out there had phoned the duty officer at the American Embassy to say that some rough-looking men armed with rifles had taken up positions in the street. When she had tried to leave the house, one of them had motioned to her to get inside — quick. It was very exciting.

Ambassador Pethwick had called a meeting of the country team for eight; all had agreed after some discussion that Washington should be put on a higher degree of alert. With more discussion it was decided that although prompt help was needed, nothing should be done to undermine confidence in Washington or in Puerto Santos in the prospects of the present government. Following the meeting of the country team and the drafting of the resulting telegram there had been a smaller meeting to review emergency procedures. This was followed by a staff meeting some part of which was devoted to discussion of the restrictions on official travel made necessary by the severe depletion of the travel budget of the Department of State. There was also a new regulation on sick leave. Now it was near noon; the telegram would soon interrupt Worth Campbell's lunch, and Ambassador Pethwick, a man of admirably regular habits, was preparing to go up to the Residence for his noonday break. Joe Hurd, a recurrent voice of pessimism at the meetings that morning, paused near the door of the Ambassador's office for a further defeatist word on the prospects for President Martínez. It was not well received, and as the two men stood talking there could be no doubt as to whose views would continue to prevail. Both were a trifle above average height. But one was well-clipped and trimmed, tanned, amply covered without being fleshy, though with a possible trace of blood pressure, and clad in well-tailored and well-pressed gray with matching tie and handkerchief. He had an air of confidence; some would say that he exuded it. The other was thin, stooped and sallow. His neck sagged away from his collar and his shoulders from the jacket. The jacket was of seersucker, the trousers of different material. Both garments were unattractive. The other man was Joe Hurd. Presently he went down to the parking lot, started his car and passed through the empty streets heading out of town. Off to the north when he slowed the car, he could hear the crack of rifles and an occasional more sustained clatter which might have been a machine gun.

The last sounds of combat that had reached Joe Hurd's ears were on Okinawa at the end of World War II. Compared with the covering fire that his company had laid down in that engagement, it was hard to think that this was serious. He seemed to recall that Latin American revolutions warmed up in the late afternoon and evening. Presently he passed a truckload of soldiers. They waved

and shouted and seemed in excellent spirits. They were
heading south. Otherwise the city looked deserted and
even more so when he turned into the great perimeter
road which, as Paseo Franklin D. Roosevelt, was started
in the prosperous years of World War II and opened by
Nelson Rockefeller in early 1945. (An extension, Avenida
Harry S Truman, was to have been ready for the world's
fair in 1950; but it was never completed, and the fair was
never held.) Paseo Roosevelt, as always, presented a
picture of disrepute and extreme disrepair. The lush
vegetation came up to the edge of the pavement, and
some straggled up through the wide-ranging cracks. At
the sides were houses of better than average aspect with
roof lines and cornices etched by light bulbs, now dull
and dark in the bright sun. In the capital of Puerto
Santos, a multitude of colored lights, not a simple red one,
denotes a brothel, and few things so please elderly North
Americans of conservative views but adventuresome dis-
position as the discovery that Paseo Roosevelt has become the whorehouse district. Modern travel turns up all
too few such conversational pearls.

Beyond the end of Paseo Roosevelt, Hurd turned between high plaster gateposts into a long private lane. He
parked the car before a large shabby house of pink stucco,
and before he had rung the bell the door was opened by
a distinguished-looking man of advanced years in a dark
worsted suit. He seemed pleased to see his visitor but
contented himself with a formal handshake. They went
out on the terrace, and presently a servant brought the
old man a small cup of coffee and Joe Hurd a large glass

of milk. Hurd's taste in beverages was evidently known.

"It is our good luck that we meet," said the old man. "I was about to leave for the club."

"So early? You once told me that you aimed for the moment between the dusk and the darkness when even the heaviest talkers pause in their day's occupation."

"You do me great honor by remembering my verse. I will not need to have it published. But this is an important day. I think we may be on the verge of great political and constitutional developments if anything in our small country can be called great."

"I would like to know."

"I believe as the deputy to your very dignified ambassador you are required to know. I think that the resistance to my friend Miró, such as it is, will probably disappear within the next few hours. I would like to be on hand when this happens. It is many years since we have had the pleasure of witnessing the inauguration of a new President in Flores. I know from my years in Washington that it is a very exciting time. I think we should have an inaugural gala and invite Mr. and Mrs. Frank Sinatra."

"You have been in touch today?"

"On that I must be noncommittal. But I do not think that Martínez's men will fight to the very bitter end. Such gestures carry no practical reward and involve an element of personal danger. Also our aging President is a man who asks much and has little left to offer."

"So there will be a deal?"

"I think there will be a deal."

Joe Hurd digested the response. Important information like good food should be savored. This was so even though it was without practical value. At the meeting that morning he had urged the likelihood of the same outcome. Pethwick had disagreed and would not now be impressed by new evidence. On the contrary, he would only suppose that some random conversation was being used as an excuse to reopen an argument that a properly disciplined subordinate should consider closed. Ambassador Pethwick was an experienced man. Presently Hurd resumed. "I heard again today that Miró is only a front — Aragón is the real power in this affair. Anyhow that is what some of our people believe."

"I have never met Sr. Aragón," said the old man, "although I have often heard his name. But there are some things you cannot do by proxy. Cooking. Painting. Making love, at least with any success. And one of these, to a singular degree, is leading a revolution — even a Latin American revolution. You can safely assume that Miró is in charge. I concede that later when it comes to running the country he will need to assert himself. As compared with throwing out Martínez that will be more difficult. Now I must insist on reciprocity in information. What are you gentlemen planning to do?"

"Your information is better than mine so you lose by the exchange. My ambassador considers Martínez a force for stability in a divided world. Washington may well agree. So they will support him. I do not agree, but this is not what we call an operational consideration."

The two men were again silent for a moment. Hurd took a sip of milk, and both looked at the ragged palms that fringed the grounds. Finally the old man spoke. "Will you intervene?"

"I don't know, and from your point of view that is no great loss for if I did I could not say. To my occasional surprise I still work for the United States government. But our first thoughts are always predictable. We have money so maybe something can be accomplished with money. We have arms so maybe arms will save the situation. A strong message of support will be forthcoming. We always have strong messages of support available. Everyone will hope that this will be enough."

"It could save Martínez," said the old man. "Not that messages of support are decisive or that he needs arms. His generals have more than enough weapons, considering the caution everyone will be exercising. But a big enough promise of money and arms could persuade our soldiers that there is more profit in the *status quo*. It could upset the deal. I use the word profit rather literally as a onetime banker. Tell me, why is Washington so willing to send Martínez arms? Does it consider him a defender of liberty and constitutional government?"

"No. It is part of what we call the larger strategy."

"So you have told me before, but this larger strategy puzzles me. Does your Pentagon think our army is an important factor in the defense of what your Secretary of State calls the free world?"

"No."

"Is it expected to play a vital part in a showdown with the armed might of the Union of Soviet Socialist Republics?"

"No."

"I am glad you show respect for the feelings of the Red Army. Do you think we are threatened by our neighbors?"

"No."

"Is it believed that our army has been the protector of our liberties here in Puerto Santos?"

"No."

"Yet you support Martínez and underwrite our army as part of the larger strategy of freedom?"

"Yes."

"I confess to wondering if you Americans always display those simple forthright qualities of mind that I used to hear praised by the more eloquent American statesmen and the late Senator Taft. I am glad you are not a defender of this local manifestation of the larger strategy."

"I'm not."

"I never imagined it, my friend. And few normally talkative men have so learned the advantages of brevity when handling impertinent questions. For my part, I still believe your great country has one redeeming quality which will save us now."

"Our idealism, it is usually said."

"No. Your untimeliness. The Austro-Hungarian monarchy was made tolerable by its inefficiency, you by your delays. Anything you do on behalf of Martínez will probably be too late. But, as a friend, I must ask you not to use this conversation as a reminder to ask Washington to expedite action."

"You have no need to worry," said the diplomat. "It

wouldn't have the slightest effect." He rose to take his leave.

•

Joe Hurd's trip back to town, once he had turned off Paseo Roosevelt, took him again through the several circles of desolation. At first on his right were Casas San Luis e San Miguel, the most publicized of the efforts of Luis Miguel Martínez to eliminate the Flores slums and indeed the only one. It had been built in the nineteen-fifties by a New Orleans contractor under the supervision of an architect who claimed to have known Robert Moses. It consisted of several acres of square concrete houses reminiscent of the machine gun emplacements that were scattered over the English countryside in World War II. Before the project was quite finished the contractor was imprisoned in the United States for income tax evasion, and the Export-Import Bank rather abruptly terminated its loan. Electricity, water and sewer pipes were never connected. Casas San Luis e San Miguel are fully occupied but in general by families who cannot find accommodations in the Flores slums. Visitors from abroad are no longer taken to see them. Joe Hurd paid them no attention nor did he much notice the slums as he passed through. The sun was high and very hot, and the small-arms fire to the north had either ceased or was out of earshot. The streets were still deserted.

3

In the center of the old city of Flores, standing by itself on one side of a wide square, is the Palace of the President. Its marble resists well both rain and sun and remains a gleaming white. When it was built in the 1920's, it was natural to look to Washington for inspiration and guidance in official architecture. But the White House seemed hardly grand enough as a model for what, recurrent democratic protestations to the contrary, had usually been the real seat of power. So the Presidential Palace was modeled on the Capitol, and the point was emphasized by giving it a dome a great deal larger in relation to the rest of the structure than its counterpart in Washington. To visitors from the United States, the building seems to be crouching under a very large white hat. Nonetheless, of all the buildings put up in Flores in this century it makes the nearest approach to an older tradition of decent public extravagance. The two houses of Congress assemble in a more modest structure, and many members have never been in it.

As night fell, President Martínez was not in his quarters in the palace. Nor was he up on the hill in the mansion of his mistresses. He was in another house, by no means small, just off Plaza Ellender in the old town. So was his mistress, though in another part of the house. And so was Manuel Pérez-Castillo, Lieutenant-General in the Army of the Republic of Puerto Santos and, perhaps, the most trustworthy of the President's supporters. He had just arrived. An aide skulked in the background. A colonel sat idly at a desk by the door and occasionally tried the telephone. Obviously it did not work.

"Our men are fighting well?" said the President. It was less a question than a way of opening the conversation, and his voice was dull.

"Under the circumstances, I would say valiantly, your Excellency."

"What do you mean, 'under the circumstances'?"

"A certain number of our officers have, unfortunately, departed."

"Deserted, you mean. They are dogs." Many years before, the President had seen the Spanish motion picture version of *A Farewell to Arms*. In fact he had seen it several times, and thereafter at first consciously and then unconsciously he had imitated the Hemingway speech. It seemed right for a roughhewn man of authority as, with very little effort, he saw himself.

The general roused himself to a response. "I agree that they are very ungrateful, Excellency. You have done much for them."

"I suppose they are now fighting bravely for Miró?"

The President allowed himself a trace of a smile as he looked at his general.

"Unquestionably, Excellency. Our men are always brave."

At his best, General Pérez did not have a quick mind, and tonight it was very tired. Possibly to sharpen it, he took another large drink of whiskey from the glass he was holding. The President reached out to do the same. Both men were sitting rather uncomfortably on gilt and brocade chairs. Both were in uniform, but the President had laid his tunic on an adjacent chair and had unbuttoned the collar of his shirt. Patches of perspiration showed on the khaki under his arms. The lights in the room flickered slightly to the beat of a generator that could be heard in a distant room. The city electricity had gone off earlier that evening. The ribbons on the President's uniform caught and reflected the light. Two of the decorations he had been awarded in Washington, one, it was said, at the behest of Dwight D. Eisenhower himself. Four had come from fellow Latin American dictators. One, the product of egregious misrepresentation extending into high Vatican circles, had been given him many years ago by the Pope. The rest, by indirection which had fooled no one, he had awarded to himself.

"How did they get the radio station?"

"It was the hour of the siesta, Excellency."

"There were no guards?"

"The attack, unfortunately, had not been foreseen."

"And the telephone exchange?"

"It is unimportant. The service was abominable."

"Stupid dogs. They would be more concerned about losing the bars and the whorehouses. What about the casualties in the fighting?"

"They have not, I am glad to report, as yet been serious."

"Mostly civilians?"

"All civilians so far, Excellency. The people have not fully obeyed instructions to remain indoors."

The conversation lagged for a moment. In the distance there was a sudden muffled burst of small-arms fire. The lights continued to flicker. From the street outside, also muffled by the thickly shuttered windows, came a shout followed by a hideous burst of laughter.

"Excellency, may I ask a question of delicacy?"

"Piss on your delicacy. I assume you want to know what I will do if the rest of those dogs desert?"

"It is reasonable, Excellency, to have what the Americans call a contingency plan."

"Fuck the Americans. That pig's ass of a Pethwick is calling on me again tonight. He will speak of the free world, urge a strong stand, promise money and guns and ask if he can report to Washington that I will resist to the last man."

"Couldn't you still ask him for some Marines to put down this foolish insurrection?"

"I have thought of it. And I have told Pethwick that the Communists are behind Miró. I told him Aragón was in charge — I think that scared them. But if their soldiers come in, I would be taking orders from one of their young generals with short hair who takes exercise and believes in the virginity of his mother. And they would talk to me about democracy and free elections. Our people do not understand democracy. I would never have been elected in a free election."

"You are right, Excellency. Could I ask again about the contingency plan?"

"Anyway, it is probably too late. I told Pethwick all we needed was weapons and some money, then we would be safe. He will have told that to Washington. I am too old to worry. I will go to Miami or Spain. Let them try democracy for a while. The ungrateful dogs, they deserve it."

"The airport is not completely available, Excellency. I fear Miró's men are also there."

"Then I will go to the Argentine and wait. He has plenty of room and doesn't talk about democracy. The Brazilian speaks Portuguese, and his wife never stops. Now it is time to get back to your men. Tell them that if they are faithful there will be promotions for everyone. There will be money from the Americans. Tell the palace guard that I am inside personally directing the defense. They will tell Miró, and that will keep the fighting down there. One must be clever in his tactics. Tell López, Santayana and Miguel to be waiting when Pethwick goes. I will send word to him later on to meet me here."

The President was speaking with some of his old fire. As a hundred times before, General Pérez found himself responding though slightly to the sense of authority strongly conveyed. But the President's fleshy jowls sagged a bit on his general's reply. And the deep folds of skin under his eyes seemed more obscene.

"I am afraid, Excellency, that none of these men are available."

·

There was still María. The President was not a reflective man, and he was not in a reflective mood; but it crossed his mind that women, at least, were loyal. He knew for he had had hundreds in his day. Some had volunteered for his bed. Some had been made available by eager parents after he had noticed them at a reception, a dinner or a ball. A contract, an army promotion, a mission to Washington, perhaps only a little deposit of good will — that was the usual price. Some came because the police had been sent to get them. But however they had arrived, they had left reluctantly. He always tried to be absent when they cried and struggled and had to be carried out. In face of such loyalty a man had to show a certain delicacy of feeling. However, for some years now there had been only María. When a man is older his mood changes — he is less interested in the novelty of firm new breasts and fresh young legs. It is better not to have to wonder if one seems old.

He opened the door to María's drawing-room without knocking.

·

There have been other nights of triumph and tragedy in the long history of Puerto de los Santos, and which they have been has depended pretty much on the point of view. Columbus is thought to have passed along the coast on his second voyage, and some even hold that he may have anchored off the little bay which was to become briefly the capital and which is now the principal port. But the undoubted father of the country was an elder son of a wealthy Spanish grandee who, in the course of a drunken brawl one night near Valladolid, was so unfortunate as to become annoyed with a favorite cousin of Queen Isabella herself. He ran the royal relative through, and then, in a singular fit of exuberance, cut off his ears, toes and testicles. Spanish manners are formal; this last, in particular, was regarded as a major breach of decorum. His family sent him on a trip to Italy, appeased the Queen by absorbing an exceptionally large share of a loan then being floated, and set about outfitting an expedition that would carry their erring offspring on a voyage of discovery to the New World. The priest who rendered holy offices for the family was receptive to the suggestion that, as a new Christian, he might easily be made vulnerable to the Inquisition, then gathering force in Castile. His uncle, it was noted, had been a distinguished rabbi. He agreed to accompany the son to insure the latter's continued spiritual health, arrange for the salvation of the souls of any aborigines that might be encountered in the new dominion, and provide a certain practical judgment which, it was feared, the son might lack.

.

Don Francisco José Francisco and his padre made a surprisingly strong team. The one broke through all barriers with impetuous and sanguinary force. The other picked up the fragments that so often remained. They crossed the Atlantic in splendid summer weather, passed into the Caribbean and, one evening just before sundown, raised the coast of Puerto Santos. For several days they worked their ship up the coast searching for a harbor and were duly grateful to God when, on another evening with a storm brewing to the south, they found their way into the bay which they appropriately named the Port of the Saints. It was now early autumn, and historians have since assumed that the storm was one side of a tropical hurricane. Off the coast they would surely have perished; in the landlocked bay they managed to ride out the great wind with two anchors although it was a near thing. The day following, they landed and, the Father having meanwhile ascertained from the notes he had made prior to his departure that the country was apparently unclaimed, they took possession in the name of Their Catholic Majesties. Mass was said, prayers of thanks were offered for the escape from the storm, and two days later the handful of Spanish horsemen put to flight or slaughtered between seven and ten thousand Indians who sought to dispute their presence or, at a minimum, to strike a reasonable bargain in return for allowing it. The pacification of the country was then complete. Further military operations were largely confined to rounding up the reluctant Indians to serve as slaves, a service that not even the hardiest survived.

The small group of white men suffered horribly during the first rainy season and a few months later removed their settlement to the higher and healthier tableland beyond. After the rainy season the site selected gleamed with large coarse red and yellow flowers and thus the name of the new capital. Not long after, Don Francisco received a message from Spain commending him for his discovery, according him full amnesty for his past transgressions, confirming him as the governor of this newest territory of New Spain and warning him solemnly of the claims of the crown to a half-share of any precious metals he might mine or take from the Indians. He never returned to Spain, and when it became clear that Puerto Santos was singularly devoid of metals, interest in the new discovery flagged in the Escorial and Seville and never really recovered. Eventually the unhealthy lowlands were converted to sugar cane, the uplands to coffee and the highest country to cattle. Men were to become as rich from these as from the mines, but, by then, Spain which, perhaps sensibly, always preferred the gold was only a distant memory. Governments came and went. There was excitement and despair, occasional hurricanes and distant economic crises which destroyed the markets for sugar and coffee. But nothing really terrible happened to Puerto de los Santos until the more or less accidental arrival of Martínez.

4

ONCE ABOUT 1949, a Pan American World Airways plane was waiting at the ramp to take off for San Juan and points south. Another was waiting to take off for Gander, Newfoundland, Shannon and London. A man came through the gate, surrendered his ticket and got on the wrong plane. The stewardess asked him his destination, but languages were not his strong suit. He thought she was asking him his name, and he replied, with pride and some emphasis, that it was Martínez. The girl was fresh from Pan Am's excellent training school in Miami and knew her duty to a passenger. She brought him a Martini, and following further efforts to check his destination and his response, several more. It was the President's younger brother Jaime, and he arrived in London very drunk at about the time that he should have reached Flores. The incident attracted a certain amount of amused newspaper comment. President Martínez shrugged it off.

The story is not untypical in the annals of the Martínez

family. Much must be attributed to accident, and much has occurred while members were under the influence of alcohol. There is nothing, incidentally, over which history draws so dense a curtain as the effect of alcohol on modern statecraft. It is agreed that it influenced the later behavior of Alexander the Great. And also numerous of the Romans. And also General Grant. In the last months of World War II, numerous of Hitler's subordinates — Ribbentrop, Ley, Funk, several of the staff officers — were consistently drunk. Thus they suppressed thought on the debacle all sober Germans saw coming. But no important military or political decision, however outrageous, is now ever explained by the fact that the man who made it was stoned. The history books are silent, even on behalf of the Nazis. Doubtless it is the conspiracy of all who worry lest they themselves will one day have to make a decision when they are one over the eight.

The Martínez dictatorship had its origins in an all-night drinking party. That was in 1932, the worst year of the Great Depression. Puerto Santos was then governed by a lawyer named Roberto Pagal, who had recently been elected in a nearly honest election. An adequate though not an adept man, Pagal faced problems that would have been taxing to a political genius. Returns from the sugar *centrales* that by then covered large areas of the lowlands were negligible. Prices for the excellent coffee that American tourists associate with breakfast in Paris, and which comes from the large *fincas* in the highlands, were halfway tolerable only because Brazil was holding so much of the world supply off the market. Cattle had no market at all — fine steaks could be had in the Flores butcher shops for the equivalent of fifteen cents a pound. Not many could afford them. The unemployed in Flores were occasionally stirred from the apathy that, more often than anger, is induced by hunger to parade with demands for bread and rice. Cane and coffee workers were raising their age-old cry for land. Landowners, including the great sugar companies that owned the cane fields, wondered by whom they would be dispossessed, their creditors or their workers, their exploiters or their exploited. Faced with a shrinking market for bananas, the United Fruit Company, whose Boston accent had long been heard with respect and sometimes with fear in Flores, began closing out its operations in the Republic. After 1933, the big white ships heading north with their cargoes of green bananas and expensively browned tourists ceased entirely to stop at Puerto Santos.

Still drunk after the night of revelry, Major Luis Miguel Martínez Obregón, thirty, and nine of his companions drove to the palace where one of their number, the Commander of the Palace Guard, ordered his men to block all further traffic through the gates. They then equipped themselves with tommy guns from the palace guardroom, arrested President Pagal while he was eating breakfast and forced him to write out his resignation, "in the interest of law, order, the stability of the currency, the defense of the Republic, a living wage for the workers, jobs for the unemployed, justice for the landless, and the fundamental security of property rights." Smarter, and by this time possibly more sober than his associates, it was Major Martínez who took these resonant terms to the new radio station and read them over the air. At the end, he thoughtfully designated himself Provisional President, announced the suspension of the Constitution, the dissolution of the Congress, and warned that resistance from whatever quarter would be dealt with firmly. That same afternoon, he named the head of the palace guard Minister of Defense and Deputy Commander-in-Chief of the Army, reserving the top military post for himself, and warned his friend that any disloyalty or undue ambition would exact a heavy price. He mentioned especially his parents, handsome wife, two children and considerable property. The following day, the American Minister came to call. The Provisional President, by now stone sober, made an excellent impression. He had no intention, he insisted, of tolerating the radical tendencies that were manifesting themselves under the previous administration. At the same time he saw his government as a temporary phenomenon; as soon as sedition had been eliminated and prosperity restored he would call for elections. A few days later, Secretary Stimson announced recognition of the new regime, and President Hoover sent an encouraging message in which he expressed his confidence in the new Martínez Administration, adding his personal conviction that prosperity was not far distant. The Minister was instructed, on delivering this message, to caution privately against any reckless or untried economic experiments.

Then began the halcyon years. Gradually, prices improved and so did government revenues and so did the supply of money that was available for the always considerable needs of the dictator. With World War II the revenues became a flood. And Washington, deeply involved with the big dictatorships in Germany, Italy and Japan, became positively benign toward the smaller ones nearer home. Martínez's new constitution did not forbid reelection; on the contrary, had the draftsman thought it permissible, it might well have recommended it. Accordingly, he was regularly reelected without opposition every four years. In conversation, he often deplored Trujillo's device of putting up a brother or a stooge through whom he ruled. Who, after all, was being fooled?

There were many more all-night parties, and now some of them had their serious side. They rewarded visiting Congressmen and Senators from the United States, including men of long tenure and great influence from the rural South in whose hearts the democratic passion is under adequate control. The result was fulsome accounts in the *Congressional Record* of the benevolence and efficiency of the friendly, staunchly anti-Communist government of Luis Miguel Martínez Obregón. Their visits created a favorable climate for the negotiation of sugar quotas — a vital matter for Puerto Santos and one on which, in the United States, members of the Agriculture Committee of the House of Representatives have jealously guarded their power and therewith the gratitude and, it is supposed, also the other rewards that are associated with favorable decisions.

President Martínez enjoyed these revels. But he never lost sight of the practical side. Once an inordinately stout legislator, being so entertained, was persuaded without difficulty to visit two professionally available young women who were on duty in an upstairs room in the Presidential Palace. When time came to go back to his hotel his trousers had disappeared and so had his undershorts. Everyone was helpful. But it was clear that so vast was the area of masculine flesh to be draped that no substitute could easily be found. While the problem was being canvassed from all angles in two languages by a highly mixed company, the Congressman became aware that someone was making a motion picture of the scene from between the railings of a balcony just above. The existence of that film, and the possibility that it might be shown in the course of a close primary contest to however few of his impoverished, illiterate, but God-fearing constituents, deeply influenced his subsequent career. Previously he had been parochial and even isolationist. Thereafter he was a man of wider horizons. Indeed, President Martínez had no more eloquent and oft-spoken partisan in all of Washington.

·

While it was a tenet of the Martínez Administration that life was worth living, it was felt that this proposition applied with special force to Martínez himself and members of his family. Accordingly, the dictator early set himself to gathering into the possession of the family nearly all of the requisites of the good life. In the flush years of World War II and after, money flowed into the treasury and on into the Martínez privy purse. And it is within the power of a dictator, in a dozen different ways, to acquire property at prices which he wishes to pay. Otherwise fire can break out in cane fields. Thieves can go unapprehended. Roads can go unrepaired — or unbuilt. Labor can become uncooperative. Or legitimate laws can be enforced and legitimate taxes collected — things no one had ever thought possible.

"But surely, señor, you are aware of the law that requires you to provide eight square meters of good housing for each of your workers?"

"You can't be serious. You would bankrupt me."

"It is little enough for a working man. And there must also be a shower and toilet."

"It is impossible! This is blackmail!"

"The fine for noncompliance is rather heavy, señor. We must also have a word one day about your back taxes. To pay taxes is both the duty and the privilege of the good citizen. That I have read."

"You will bankrupt me!"

"Perhaps you would like to realize on your holdings while . . ."

·

In the years between 1940 and 1960, all of the best sugar lands passed into the hands of the Martínez family, and all five mills where the cane is ground. So did the worthwhile coffee *fincas*. The larger cattle ranches were bought by agents of the President and also the bauxite deposit, to which the Canadians eventually obtained a concession. The Martínez family came to own the cement plant, much real estate in downtown Flores and Puerto Santos, the largest trucking company, the bus line, part of the airline, and through a variety of fronts the import franchises for a score or more of the popular brands of American and European automobiles, trucks, cigarettes, whiskey, camera film, cloth, Colas, radios, pharmaceuticals and building materials. Little remained. Juan, the favorite son of the President and by a wide margin the most devoted, serious and responsible of his acknowledged offspring, was studying recondite subjects of social consequence at the University of Michigan on a bribe, more or less adequately disguised as a scholarship, from a large American oil firm of unquestioned rectitude. This was in return for participation in a marketing firm owned nominally by Jaime Martínez — he of the unscheduled journey — and the monopoly privileges invariably enjoyed by any Martínez firm. In acquiring property, President Martínez had learned a good deal from his contemporaries, Generals Trujillo and Somoza. But avid and expert though these dictators were, as collectors of capital assets, they could have learned a thing or two from Martínez. In an unexpected and somewhat unusual way this wealth contributed to his undoing.

.

The bearing of the Martínez wealth on the survival of the regime, was, oddly enough, the subject of discussion at the Santos Club — the Club, possibly misnamed, of the Saints — on the night that his enemies closed in on the dictator.

Many think this building, on the square opposite the cathedral, the most beautiful in Flores, and possibly in what was once New Spain. The main structure dates from colonial times, but it was greatly extended and improved early in the present century when rich sugar and coffee planters, Flores merchants and an occasional cattleman felt a need for a congenial resort where they might restore themselves after a lonely vigil on their land or a long day in the counting room. In those days, neither politicians nor army officers were allowed to belong, and the barrier has never been entirely lifted. However, in recent times, it has been understood that if the President of the Republic insists, a man must be admitted. This has not often happened, and the club has never been popular with the Martínez regime.

In inspiration the club is Venetian not Spanish, and the high chaste walls with the scalloped fringe along the top are solid and have withstood well the rains. So has the great nail-studded door although its metal has not been polished for many years and has tarnished to a dull green. Within, the red tile floors are laid on a thick footing of mortar and crushed rock and are still level, cool and clean. There is more than a trace of grandeur in the large central patio to which the building is open and which it seems to surround almost as an afterthought. The chairs are angular and solid, the seats are large sheets of leather and from the heavy refectory tables one imagines that monks might eat. It is all shabby but still very strong and beautiful. The bar is fully fifty feet long, and the occasional visitors are still shown a bullet hole where the bullet is still lodged after passing through the alleged seducer of the daughter of a rich and angry coffee planter. Acting on a hasty and rather general description, the rancher had shot the leading Flores pharmacist by mistake. Visitors are less likely to be shown the table where, in the late twenties, the American Minister drank himself to death. A former Republican State Chairman from South Dakota, his pleasure in his unexpected escape from prohibition knew no bounds. Once he solemnly mounted the bar and announced his intention of riding it all the way back to Sioux Falls. The stories of his final delirium are of slight clinical interest and not entirely pleasant, but his widow gave a handsome stained-glass window to the Protestant chapel in his honor. Nor do members like to recall the more recent occasions when the Martínez police have entered to arrest a member suspected of plotting against the regime, or whose sudden departure, it had been decided, would be a useful warning to those who probably were.

The number of such arrests has not been large, for the club in recent times has not had many members. The rich and the well-to-do who once graced its rolls are those, naturally enough, who aroused the acquisitive instinct of Martínez. They are gone from Puerto Santos, and those who wish to get along under the regime find the club of no help. Once the bar featured every alcoholic beverage known to the Americas — tequila, pisco sour, planter's punch, *aguardiente*, whiskey sour with bourbon, scotch and soda, gin and tonic, Jack Daniels, Four Roses, Schlitz. Now the single aging waiter searches under the bar for a bottle and shuffles out to the kitchen for some ice. The food is far from good and frequently, and for good reason, has a warmed-over taste. None of the regular patrons is under sixty, but for a score or so beyond this age it is a much-loved link with a much better past. They will be sorry when, as all recognize must eventually happen, the club finally closes its doors.

·

On this night none of the shabbiness and only a little of the beauty of the club were visible, for here too the electricity was off. And only indistinctly visible in the light reflected from the half-moon rising in the night sky were the two elderly men who sat at a table in the big patio. One seemed to be rather somberly dressed in what might have been dark tropical worsted. The other was in crumpled white. There were some sounds of movement from the direction of the bar or kitchen; otherwise they were alone. Neither had spoken for several minutes, but finally the man in dark observed: "It seems that the firing has stopped."

"I expect Martínez has things under control," his companion replied. "Anyway, we will know soon enough. I realize that you have a contrary opinion."

"Contrary and, I believe, correct," the man in dark replied. "Martínez is finished. It is only that it has taken a certain time for people to make this interesting and important discovery."

"I have still to be persuaded. He has soldiers. He has police. Both impress me. I confess to regretting the temperament which caused me to accept your invitation to join you here tonight. Besides there is very little to see."

"Don't be alarmed. Age is a great protection. Men do not respect years, but they instinctively feel that with a little patience the appropriate punishment will come from other and more authoritative sources. Why waste energy or run risk for what the Lord will accomplish in a few years? So we are spared." The man in dark took a sip from a glass or cup, put it back on the table and listened to the sounds beyond the walls for a moment. There were distant shouts but still no shooting. He continued in a rather didactic tone.

"You would be more sanguine, I believe, if you understood the nature of power. And exceptional too, for in my experience it is not even understood by those who wield it. There is, of course, the power of love, which, in the case of Luis Martínez, can reasonably be excluded. For the rest, it is merely a matter of reward and punishment. Men can pay others to accept their will or they can punish them for failing to do so. These are the sources of power, and it is a remarkable fact that when the ability to reward disappears so does the ability to punish. Martínez has now lost both. Accordingly, he will disappear, and, in my view, that will happen this evening."

"You are eloquent and logical as always, my friend. But I fail to see why Martínez is so suddenly assailed by this weakness."

"It was not sudden. He has been living on borrowed

time, and any serious opposition was certain to topple him. Fairly certain, perhaps I should say. Once the members of this club were rich and numerous and most of them wanted to be richer still. Their wealth and their avarice were the source of the Martínez power to punish and reward. They did his bidding lest he take away their money or their chance to make more. Thus his power of punishment. And he could take away enough to give other people jobs, graft and trips to the United States. Thus his power to reward. Now the wealth is gone, the people are gone and the taxes are gone. Is it surprising that his power has also gone?"

"How can you say that the wealth has gone? It was merely stolen by Martínez. That you know."

"That I have personal reason to know, but let us not quibble at this hour of the night. It earns him little. A man who relies on gangsters, gunmen and rascals to protect his person cannot get honest men to manage his property. Those who run the Martínez *centrales* and *fincas* are scoundrels to a man. They make him no money and would not share it if they did. Do you suppose that Captain Kidd, when he graced our shores, returned much revenue to his owners?"

"Martínez has the police."

"Another case where you can only have punishment if you can pay. Even putting a red-hot knitting needle up a man's penis is not, for everyone, an intrinsically attractive pastime. Most must be paid for such craftsmanship and promised promotions and made to feel that they are part of a going concern. Otherwise efficiency suffers.

I admit there are unselfish exceptions who do this work for its own sake. Happily, they are few."

"He has money from the Americans."

"I admit that the Americans are a problem. They are defending freedom and resisting Communism, and it is a great tragedy when this takes place in a small country like ours with a dictator like Martínez. We have not been the first so to suffer. But I think it is now too late even for the American money. Also, others have been saying that they could get more. But pardon me, I wonder if the revolution isn't approaching our door."

The old man got up and listened again. There were still no shots, but unmistakably there was a sound of crowded footsteps and occasional shouts and commands outside. Presently there was a pounding on the door. "Perhaps you will excuse me. I made certain arrangements for our friends to use the club as a command post, possibly even as a place of detention. It was good of you to keep me company. I trust that my predictions are sound and that they are not seeking asylum." The old man disappeared into the darkness in the direction of the door. Presently flashlights and then a lantern pierced the gloom.

5

AT THE UNIVERSITY OF MICHIGAN at Ann Arbor earlier that afternoon, August Schmiltz, Charles E. Sorenson Distinguished Public Service Professor of Political Science, had taught his regular afternoon class in Constitutional and Political Development. For graduate students he was a firm believer in the Socratic method, although this belief was diluted somewhat by a conflicting commitment to autobiography. During the course of the two-hour session, he had adverted at some length to his role in the writing of the constitution of the state of Württemberg-Baden while serving with John J. McCloy in Germany after World War II. This was followed by a more detailed account of the political advice that, a few years later, he had given President Kwame Nkrumah of Ghana, all of which the latter, to his ultimate sorrow, had wholly ignored. Not sensing that he was losing his audience, Professor Schmiltz had then discussed the bearing of the revolution of rising expectations and certain other revolutions on the stability of constitutional regimes. He noted that individual liberties were secure only under a system of social justice and emphasized that the Communists had never, in the course of a free election, succeeded in voting themselves into power. The class continued to show marked signs of apathy. Then Professor Schmiltz paused for a moment, and a student put up his hand. The others looked across the waste of blond plywood seats — the classroom was far from crowded — with mild interest. Perhaps there would be a moment's escape from boredom. None could recall ever having heard this particular scholar ask a question before. It was Juan César Martínez, son of the embattled dictator of Puerto de los Santos. Perhaps in some distant way the knowledge, filtered in small paragraphs through the Detroit papers, of the struggle that was in progress in his home country led him to speak. He had never spoken in class before; not many knew his name.

"Do you think, sir, that the New Left might succeed where the Old Left failed?"

Attention returned to Schmiltz, but only briefly. Richly and often excessively informed on the past, or such of it as had benefited from his association, he was less in touch with the present. The New Left, the New Politics, the Maoist revival, students for democratic and other societies — he could not bring himself to take any of them seriously. In fact, he did not know what they were. He looked genially at his class and at his interlocutor and replied: "In the last analysis I think we can count on the eventual triumph of the free spirit. I will tell you why . . ." Before he had finished the class had ceased to listen.

·

While the revolution was moving to its climax in Puerto Santos, everyone in Washington had been attending meetings. These had begun early in the afternoon following the arrival of Pethwick's telegram. No one had mistaken its note if not of urgency at least of disturbed expectation. First there was an important session with the military and CIA on the contingency plan in the event of an open attempt at a Communist take-over. The AID, USIA, Treasury, the Bureau of the Budget, and Agriculture came together in Worth Campbell's office to discuss a package which, hopefully, would shore up and save the Martínez regime. At five o'clock word came that the President could meet with them that evening. Worth Campbell had thereupon authorized a telegram to Pethwick telling him that he could assure Martínez that Washington was responding with urgency to his problem. Something concrete could be expected within another twelve to twenty-four hours. Pethwick could not reveal what the help would be, but he could say that help was on the way. The difference was not vital.

·

Worth Campbell also had a word with his wife. It wouldn't be worthwhile coming home for dinner. She used the occasion to express a usual word of worry about their son. But her husband knew that, worried or not, in accordance with a custom dating to the earliest and most contented of their married years, she would immediately after dinner go promptly to bed. The wives of other hard-working or great men felt obliged to keep themselves in a condition of compassionate strain. Loretta May Campbell's solution was different; she merely got a lot of sleep.

With everything, it was nearly seven when Campbell came out of the air-conditioned climate of the State Department into the unaccustomed heat of the city. As always, it seemed to take one in physical embrace. He walked only a block or two before taking a cab to the Occidental, the best restaurant within reach of the White House.

There are men whom headwaiters recognize instantly as important. There are others, including many important ones, who invariably dine with the door of the men's room hitting their elbow and to the sound of running water. Worth Campbell, perhaps as a result of his rimless glasses, perhaps because he had need to look impressive only from behind a desk, was one of the latter. He had often noticed it. Now he was banished to a back table in the inside room immediately below a picture of Senator Arthur Capper of Kansas. The waiter took his order. His judgment as to the guest's essential inconsequence was a trifle shaken when Campbell declined a drink. In Washington eccentricity often suggests importance. In fact, Worth Campbell was untroubled by the seclusion; for a second time, he found himself, and with the same twinge of annoyance, feeling that his eating arrangements were not quite right. As it had been improper on this day of crisis to have lunch with too many people, now it was slightly odd that he should be dining all alone. After considering Capper for a moment, he glanced at the hundreds of other photographs of Washington statesmen lining the walls. Most of them were legislators; the legislative, as compared with the executive or judicial personality, goes better with a restaurant wall. Men of more speculative mind might have reflected on the criteria for selection: Eloquence? Leadership? Notoriety? Long tenure in office? The ability to write one's name? If the building survived Washington redevelopment, some men would one day have to go, for very little space remained. Presumably spectacular contribution and imaginative wickedness would triumph over dull virtue or routine sin. George Norris and Joe McCarthy could stay. The elder Wagner and Styles Bridges would eventually go. Worth Campbell was not a man to care. He came back to Senator Capper, and his mind shifted from his own dining habits to legislators in general and then to the events of the afternoon.

For quite a few Foreign Service Officers the legislators along the walls are, second only to the Communists, the prime enemy of American foreign policy. This is an attitude derived in part from ignorance and in part from fear. Worth Campbell had encountered men who would face with equanimity a mob howling for the glass of an American Embassy or the books of an American library but who dissolved in fear at the thought of a congressional committee, even a friendly one. Before it, they became either totally tongue-tied or sought to confess the most ghastly defects of character and the most improbable derelictions of duty in order to disarm their inquisitors. Worth Campbell was too experienced for this. And while, as an expert, he was naturally uneasy at the way Congressmen, the most congenital of amateurs, passed judgment on matters that even a professional found complicated, his discontent this evening centered on the Executive Branch. It was severe, and it embraced especially the people with whom he had done business that afternoon.

The meeting with the military had been all right. They had long ago defined the enemy, and they were not given to doubt. Some of their proposals for action, inevitably, were crude. But it was their business to propose and that of the civilian to moderate and decide. They were more sensible than most civilians supposed. They were a lot more inclined to be guided by hard experience.

The trouble had begun at the second meeting when a middle-aged man from AID — by his manner and speech Worth Campbell judged that he might be a new recruit from a Midwestern university — had questioned the whole idea of support for Martínez. "I am not an authority on this country," he had said, "but it strikes me that we aren't getting very much for our investment. Do we really think Martínez is a paying proposition?" Worth Campbell thought he identified the liberal who disguised left-wing ideas in tough business language, and the next words were a giveaway. "If there is any real program for the average citizen down there, anything that reflects the social aims of the *Alianza,* I haven't seen it. On the record, I would be in favor of ringing the bell."

Bill O'Donnell had looked pleased, and before Worth Campbell could respond, the USIA man sounded forth. How could we be serious about supporting a man like Martínez? It made complete hash of anything we said in Latin America about liberty and freedom or even common honesty in government. "I would just about as soon have to sell Stalin." The fellow was young and good-looking and spoke easily as though he were announcing a news program. A young lawyer from the Legal Adviser's office, who was present only to comment on the sugar quotas, nodded enthusiastic assent. Again, of course, did Bill O'Donnell. For a brief moment Worth Campbell had wondered if they were in collusion. He decided there wouldn't have been time to conspire, but he moved sharply, nonetheless, to end the nonsense.

"There are probably better men in Puerto Santos than Martínez. I don't like his kind of government any better than you do. After all, I was brought up to believe in democracy too. There is no difference between us on that. But we've also got to be practical. Martínez is in office. Those who would serve our interests better are not in office, and we don't even know who they are." The Assistant Secretary had let his small eyes behind their rimless glasses move from one to another of those present before driving home his point.

"I don't know who they are; and no one in this room can give me the name of a man we can back and be sure of getting into office, and whose performance he will guarantee once in power. We do know what kind of people would like to take over. Under these circumstances what do we do? I say again, gentlemen, we have to be practical. We have to support Martínez, and we know it."

It was a good speech, but it may not have been what carried the day. In the bureaucracy it is superior position reinforced by certainty of manner which wins. These Worth Campbell possessed. Argument, even eloquence, provides only the grace notes for what, otherwise, would seem a too naked exercise of authority. When Worth Campbell had spoken, they got down to business. What could be done?

Nevertheless Worth Campbell had not liked this insurrection. It was symptomatic of a problem that increasingly troubled him — the inability of a younger generation to learn from the experience which had provided such bitter lessons to his own. Some even seemed unaware that there were lessons to be learned. Worth Campbell was not given to nostalgia. But he thought often of the days when things were better understood.

·

In particular, this had been true in his years in Paris following World War II. He had earned these years for himself during the war. In Washington it is well understood that great men are great only because of the efforts of lesser men who help bear the drudgery of greatness. Greatness requires that speeches be written, congressional testimony be prepared, and that those so endowed be briefed for meetings, coached on urgent needs before visits to the White House and be minimally informed before seeing the press. Great men must be told what action will enrage congressmen, labor leaders, businessmen or bureaucrats, for not even the greatest man can be forewarned by his own sense of caution on all of these things. A great man must, when he leaves for an inescapable re-

ception, dinner, cocktail party or a weekend of much
needed rest, have someone who will check drafts, get sig-
natures, inform legislators, appease rival departments,
clear press releases and otherwise tidy up the dozens of
other details that make operative the smallest act of statecraft. Great men on occasion have mistresses, debts or un-
speakable tendencies for which reticence must be arranged. Washington during the war was full of great men
and, accordingly, the men who sustained greatness were at
a premium. None sustained it so completely and with such
self-effacement as Worth Campbell. During the war he
served on the War Production Board, and Donald Nelson,
Charles Wilson and Ferdinand Eberstadt, though impeccable in their personal habits, all admitted their debt to
this devoted and extremely efficient young man. They
paid him the supreme tribute: "There were times when
that young fellow saved my life." After the war, Campbell
returned to teaching, found it dull, and presently one of
the great men with whom he had served in Washington
invited him to Berlin to join the occupation staff of General Lucius Clay. Then came the Marshall Plan, and many
great men came to Paris. Here the need for support to
greatness was no less than in Washington. By now Worth
Campbell had also a good working knowledge of Europe.
He went to Paris and, like so many others temporarily in
that city, found that these were to be the best years of his
life.

The Maison Talleyrand on the Rue de Rivoli was then
the historic and rather shabby headquarters of the European Cooperation Administration. Not since the Caro-

lingian Empire had any single structure been so recognizably the center of Europe. In company with the most noted men of the time, Worth Campbell was engaged in the most important work of the time which was saving the western world from international Communism. The enemy was as real as and in many ways more dangerous than the field-gray legions which had ravaged Europe fewer than five years before. But now, in defense, it was not the rude methods of the soldier but the subtler techniques that flowed from expert civilian understanding that were required. And this Worth Campbell provided.

During the thirties, as a graduate student and teaching assistant, Worth Campbell had maintained a measure of scholarly reserve toward the political excitements of the time. A scholar does not go overboard for Communism, socialism, the Spanish Republic, the CIO or John Maynard Keynes. He must remain in position to ask questions. Campbell's reserve had commended itself to the senior professors in his department at a time when jobs were scarce. He was advanced over more spectacular performers of less good judgment.

His reserve continued during the war years and immediately after. His contemporaries invested their emotional, spiritual and political capital in the idea of a permanent association with Britain and the Soviets. They worked on plans for the United Nations or they became involved with UNRRA and China and Yenan. Worth Campbell remained with materials allocations and conservation orders and reconversion planning and getting Germany going again. As one consequence, when security checks were inaugurated in the late forties, and thereafter when the witch-hunts began, he confronted them not only with a perfect record but with a perfect conscience. Not many men of his education and experience could claim as much. Knowing the care it had required to keep himself clear of entanglements, it was reasonable for Worth Campbell to conclude that, in contrast with so many of his contemporaries, he had always enjoyed a deeper insight into the nature of the Communist conspiracy. In the public service, as perhaps elsewhere, the most important factor in the assessment of a man is the assessment he offers of himself. So it was with Worth Campbell. Increasingly, he viewed himself as a foresighted and penetrating strategist in the great confrontation of the free world and Communism. Increasingly, this view was accepted by others. Cabinet officers in Paris for a few days, junketing legislators assailed by a sudden need to display social purpose, Joseph and Stewart Alsop, John Foster and Allen Dulles, Thomas E. Dewey, Eric Johnston, Winthrop Aldrich, erstwhile academic colleagues who had once urged upon Campbell the need to understand the aspirations of the Soviet Union now sought him out or were brought into his office by the great men to be briefed. Later at the Ritz or the Crillon or the Georges V or, in the case of the professors, at mean little hostels on the *rive gauche* labeled by the knowing as "simple but not good," the visitors told each other or their wives that Worth Campbell was a man who had things taped.

·

Other things in these years added to his understanding of the world and the enemy with which he was contending. In Paris Worth Campbell kept his social life strictly subordinate to duty, and in a day when many other men were using service with the Economic Cooperation Administration as a sabbatical year from a depressing business, university or Washington routine, this too added to his value. But not even the devoted Dr. Campbell was wholly indifferent to the official and semi-official rewards of life in Paris in this heady time. He enjoyed the long business luncheons and the intimate dinners over good food that discussed the future of European unification. Worth Campbell gradually became known as a man who could be counted upon to put forward fairly bold ideas — the enactment of antitrust laws as an aid to European free enterprise, the enforcement of a non-Communist oath in the European unions, extension of American methods of management-labor cooperation, better marketing methods for European industry. At a hundred meetings he developed these ideas.

Of other aspects of Paris life he deliberately saw less. When visiting firemen proposed an after-dinner tour of the nudes and whores of the Place Pigalle, he invariably pleaded work. Sometimes he had work, and sometimes he went home to his sleeping wife. He listened to the veiled accounts of such adventures without obvious regret.

Once in the summer of 1949, when his wife and boys were back in Maryland for the holidays, he went to a reception for Christian Herter who was visiting Paris.

There he fell into conversation with the wife of a French colleague, an *Inspecteur des Finances* with whom he had recently served on a working party on the European Payments Union. She was well-groomed, voluble and quite good-looking, and with her husband shared a wide and eclectic acquaintance in French political life. He was known to have advanced rapidly in his career under the *Front Populaire,* and he had been active in the *Résistance.* She told him she too was a summer widow; her husband had just left on another extended trip to Hanoi. He asked her to dinner.

They went to dinner and afterward to her flat for coffee and brandy. It was extremely pleasant, and she spoke in fascinating and sometimes clinical detail of her wartime success in seducing German intelligence officers. Later, pleading the need for relaxation, she changed to flowing white silk pajamas, the *ao dai* that men bring their wives from Indo-China, and a very little later she invited Worth Campbell, with astonishing frankness, to remain and make love. She had no difficulty in discovering that he had at least contemplated the same possibility and commented colorfully on the phenomenon. He escaped with no small pride in his self-discipline and a heightened awareness of the vulnerability of the basic design of men's pants. He never doubted that she had something more than sex in mind. He continued to be grateful for his self-control although not completely so.

In time the great men went home. So eventually did Worth Campbell. The Republicans came in, and he worked a while for Dulles. He was respected, and all the more since he had voted for Ike, but he was no longer quite at the center. Eventually he agreed to become director of the Institute for International Affairs at his old university. Castro turned Campbell's attention to Communism in Latin America, and when the Democrats returned, his old friends mentioned him as a man who should be used. He could serve a function but little understood in liberal administrations. These administrations need liberals for domestic tasks — not even a moderate conservative can be Secretary of Labor or of Health, Education and Welfare. But for foreign policy it is essential to have men who inspire confidence. This liberals do not do. Unless immediately on taking office they allay suspicion by taking an exceptionally strong stand in the Cold War, they will be suspected of a tendency, however subjective, toward appeasement of the Communists. The smallest gesture of conciliation will confirm this mistrust. Accordingly, liberal administrations must put conservatives in charge of foreign policy or, best of all, nonpolitical experts. Thus their need for men like Worth Campbell. Unconsciously over the years Campbell had come to think of something resembling his own background and political attitude as the basic qualification for making foreign policy. Others he too regarded as interlopers.

.

"Are you going over to the meeting, sir?" A young man with dark hair, lean face and black unpressed suit had come up beside Worth Campbell's table. Evidently he had been dining in the other room and had seen the Assistant Secretary come in. He was a former research fellow in Campbell's Institute and had served for a year as assistant to the director. Thereafter, abandoning political neutrality, he had written campaign speeches and was now in the White House. His duties included an indistinct responsibility for Latin America. There was no man in Washington whose existence Worth Campbell resented more. It was not the difference in age; all who survive in that city accustom themselves sooner or later to taking instruction from men young enough to be their own sons and seemingly less wise. Campbell's resentment traced to a Saturday morning several years before when he had gone into his deserted office at the Institute to look at his mail. One of the envelopes he opened was an application for a senior fellowship. The applicant, evidently a friend of his assistant, had, inexplicably, included a letter from the latter along with his own application form, *curriculum vitae* and letters of recommendation. The letter which his assistant had written read in part:

You will have to be braced for our Director. He is in some ways quite an intelligent man. If you are interested in strengthening NATO, strategy on Berlin, European unification, the MLF, other nuclear arrangements to please the Germans, and the history of the Marshall Plan, you couldn't do better. But don't get him on to anything very modern. He doesn't want the world to change and he doesn't want the Communists to change and he is secretly annoyed, I think, by their disagreements. We are still having quite a rugged Cold War around here . . .

Campbell had never let it be known that he saw the letter. But he had not forgotten it; and when the FBI came investigating his former assistant for his present post, he had wondered what was his duty. He had contented himself with a comment on a certain immaturity of judgment. Perhaps as a simple exercise of responsibility he should have said more. He did not forget the letter now as he paid his bill and they walked out onto Pennsylvania Avenue, across in front of the grave classical facade of Treasury and along the high iron fence which circled the White House grounds to the south. Nor had he altogether dismissed it from mind by the time they reached the barrier at the lower end of West Executive Avenue where the Secret Service officer examined his credentials and waved his young companion through.

6

THE WHITE HOUSE, more than any other building that comes to mind, has a personality that differs depending on the door by which it is entered. Each weekday morning some thousands of tourists come up by the Treasury and stream in through the East Wing. For them it is a place of wide, shadowed basement corridors, handsome staircases, large empty rooms, portraits of Lincoln, and blue-uniformed Secret Service men with large gold badges who bar the way to the deeper recesses and, rather surprisingly, have the solid, settled, unathletic appearance of a branch bank manager or a professor of public speaking. For many it is a memorable experience. Some feel slightly let down.

For all who enter the center doors, either south or north, the lovely mansion is merely the backdrop for a glittering assemblage and the ear-splitting music of a brilliantly uniformed military band. It is a self-conscious assemblage. No woman is ever present who does not show the extra effort that has gone into her hair, makeup and dress.

For some the effort has been too evidently excessive. It suggests art, not beauty. And not even the most jaded couple are indifferent to the fact that they, among so many in the Republic, have been selected to be there. None, in speech or manner, quite succeeds in concealing this self-regard. It is told that once the magnificent new wife of a washing machine magnate attended such a White House gala in an exceptionally low-cut evening gown. While conversing expansively with an elderly Senator, her breasts fell out. She did not notice, the difference being not excessive, and so intent were they on themselves that neither did any of the men or more than a handful of the other women. Eventually they were replaced by a secretary to the President's wife who was mildly reproved by the lady for an unnatural act.

For those who, like Worth Campbell and his companion, come in through the West Basement to the West Wing, the White House is a place of official toil. Work in the West Wing goes on either in the cheerful spaciousness of the President's oval office or the more somber opulence of the cabinet room, and here everyone who speaks is aware that his remarks may one day be a part of the history of the era or, better still, by the depth of their perception, their ingenuity in dissipating perplexity, or their extreme solidity of conventional good sense so impress the President that, thereafter, the speaker will be a man of even greater influence. Or work proceeds, not in these rooms of state, but in a very small conference room on the top floor of the small building or in one of the modest offices of the President's assistants which open off the narrow shabby corridors. Here men speak with less restraint. And here ideas become proposals, and proposals become plans, and plans are firmed up and reduced to paper, and papers are revised and then reconsidered and, as the product of this parturition, emerge as presidential speeches, messages to Congress, draft legislation, press releases, Executive Orders, communications to the heads of other states or instructions to ambassadors or generals operating in distant lands. It is only dimly understood even in Washington how much power this process reposes in the few who are able to translate thought into typable words in the presence of a dozen or more eager, articulate but largely unlettered colleagues. And those who enjoy this power are careful not to let its extent be known, for it would mean closer scrutiny of their drafts.

.

It was from such a drafting session that the two officials now emerged. Earlier in the evening there had been a session with the President. When that was over, those present sat down to record the results in what Washington, concealing affection with contrived casualness of language, always calls a piece of paper and to agree on the wording of a presidential message of support to Martínez. The Secretary could, with decency, have gone home earlier, but even his worst critics have never said that he is other than a conscientious man. The Assistant Secretary had, of course, to remain to the end. So did most of the others.

It had not been an abnormally difficult evening. White

House meetings are usually not. Except for the presidential assistants, they are attended only by principals. The higher the officials, the less talk tends to be an end in itself, the more a prelude to agreement and action. First there had been some discussion of the proper course of action if Martínez collapsed and the Communists tried to take over. Then, suiting assumption to the preferred course of history, they had settled down to ways and means of saving Martínez. The Chairman of the Joint Chiefs was currently inspecting bases on some distant sector of the nation's defense perimeter. His deputy, a close student of professional prose, had stated the position of the military. "If this man is in trouble down there and he's on our side, I'd be in favor of going in with sufficient force to help him out. There's no substitute for doing what it takes." The President had listened gravely and with every indication of approval. But then with the air of a man who must regularly eschew the straightforward, logical course had replied, "I don't think it has come to quite that stage yet." The general had smiled agreeably. He had entertained no expectation that his recommendation would prevail. The pleasure was in making it.

There was more trouble from the White House staff who, all too obviously, had also been instructing the President. They wanted to know if Martínez was worth saving. He was a dictator; his own people were against him; he was unpopular in the rest of Latin America; he was organically retarded in all economic matters. The *Alianza* had promised democratic government and a better life for the average man; Martínez was interested in a better life only for Martínez. In short, he was deficient on all known counts. This came in snatches from the President and more volubly from his men. It was a routine objection, but still it had to be met. Worth Campbell met it as he had already that day, but with rather less vehemence. He did not deny the facts; he deplored them, as did all, but stressed the unfortunate operational superiority of the devil you know. Martínez had governed the country for a long while. Better a while longer than a blind plunge into a dangerous unknown. The President, he felt sure, would not wish another Communist dictatorship, another Castro, in that part of the world. He and the Secretary, for better or worse, had the responsibility for protecting the President. Worth Campbell rather enjoyed making this point in the presence of the President's staff, but no one there could have guessed it. In the end, the proposals of the afternoon meeting in Campbell's office were accepted though with some reduction in expense. The President went off to the mansion remarking that crises in American foreign policy seemed always to be resolved in the same way: a strong letter from him accompanied by a large check. There was an appreciative laugh.

The drafting session had been somewhat more troublesome. Worth Campbell owed much of his success in the bureaucratic jungle to his skill at quietly taking over when this stage was reached. But his former assistant had also learned a thing or two. He was aided by the Byzantine protocol of Washington which gives the drafting of presidential letters not to the ablest or most experienced man at a meeting or the one of most majestic rank, but to any presidential assistant who is there. This assistant was determined to include some language calling for liberalization of the Martínez regime — land reform, elections, prompt trials for those in jail for political crimes, possibly a curb on the police. Laboriously this had to be batted down. However appropriate in a speech, however valuable as a declaration of principles by the Organization of American States, these things did not belong in a letter of encouragement and support. This must have practical force; extraneous material could only dilute the effect.

The general had broken a long silence to come to Worth Campbell's support. "When I'm ordering a bunch of my boys to get in there and fight, I don't go telling them they're out of uniform." Eventually a fairly strong and quite sensible letter had been agreed upon. Worth Campbell and the Secretary walked by the desk of the Secret Service man at the door of the basement and stepped out into West Executive Avenue ahead of the others. It was around eleven. Elsewhere events were taking their course, sometimes independently of strategy being devised in the capital of the free world.

·

The two men paused at the curb, looking across the narrow street at the dark bulk that in more innocent days had housed the State, War and Navy Departments and now no longer quite accommodates the numerous appendages of the White House.

"Do you think it will work?" It was the Secretary who spoke, and the question had a routine, conversational sound.

"Well, it's a package. The only thing we can do at the moment is to maintain the dialogue with Martínez and stiffen his defenses and morale."

"I agree. The dialogue is certainly important . . . God! Some of these younger men." It was about as far as the Secretary ever went either in profanity or criticism of his colleagues in government, and even then he unconsciously looked over his shoulder.

"They may learn some day that in this world you have to do business with some pretty unpleasant people."

"I hope so. I sometimes wonder why writing campaign speeches or teaching torts or literary history at Harvard or some university qualifies a man as an expert on foreign policy."

"There is still no proof that it does, Mr. Secretary."

"I gather that was one of your old students who was proposing that we instruct Martínez on the ways of reform."

"My assistant, in fact. I have always tried to keep the world safe for diversity." It was not often that Worth Campbell joked about serious matters. Even now he sounded a trifle forced.

"Well, it's the government," said the Secretary. "Are you reasonably certain that Martínez can make it?"

"We both know about the people who are waiting if he doesn't, Mr. Secretary. We grew up in the same school."

"How much confidence do you have in Pethwick?" Just

perceptibly the Secretary had lowered his voice. There is no subject as avidly discussed in Washington as the competence of third persons. But in the State Department it is understood that ambassadors are to be treated with some special reverence, and the Secretary of State tried to set an example.

"He is solid, and he is no starry-eyed amateur. After tonight we can appreciate that advantage. He has also been through the mill and knows the kind of people we're fighting. But we don't send men like Chip and Tommy to places like Puerto Santos."

"Well, let's hope for the best. I sometimes think that is what I get paid for doing. You got transportation, Worth?"

"They called me a White House car. I've got to get this stuff off to Pethwick. Some of my boys are standing by."

"You can't telephone Flores?"

"Lord, no. Martínez has all the overseas lines passing through the palace. He would listen in himself if he were up to the language."

"Well, I've heard that there is some wiretapping in this democracy. See you in the morning." The Secretary motioned to his chauffeur, and the latter opened the door of the car. The Secretary waved a hand to Campbell as he settled into the seat.

Campbell watched the Cadillac pull away, purr gently as it passed up the short street, pause almost imperceptibly at the barrier at Pennsylvania Avenue and then, its lights cutting a momentary swath across the trees and grass of Lafayette Park, turn down the nearly empty ave-

nue. The White House car, a black Mercury, was pulling
up to the curb. The others were now coming out the door.

•

Bill O'Donnell, Symes Jones, Deputy Assistant Secretary for Inter-American Affairs, and a well-tailored young
man whom Worth Campbell could not immediately place
were waiting in an outer room of the Assistant Secretary's
office.

"Anything in from Pethwick?" Campbell asked as he
caught sight of his men.

"Just an acknowledgment of your last message telling
him we'd have something for him tomorrow," Bill O'Donnell replied. "The CIA has a flash from the man they just
sent down. The shooting seems to have died down, and
the city is fairly quiet. I expect he's out around the cat
houses by now trying to find out what happened. How
did the meeting go?"

"Well, we have a package." As though he spoke literally, the Assistant Secretary tossed the manila envelope
that he was carrying on the table. "It is pretty much as
we worked it out. Some trimming. Ten million for new
budget support. Same for new arms — small arms, riot
control, ammunition, some quartermaster stuff. Military
advisers. Stepped up counter-insurgency training for
their army. Some helicopters for greater mobility. A
strong letter pledging personal support from the President
himself to Martínez. The Pentagon is developing a new
contingency plan."

"What would you say was the general reaction of the

President?" Symes Jones was training himself in the use of precise professional speech.

"I can't say he was very happy about it."

"What would you say was his principal reservation?"

"The money. The money. His boys had also given Martínez a pretty bad billing, although maybe no worse than he deserves. And, of course, he wanted to know why we hadn't foreseen this trouble. I told him you had, Bill."

The Assistant Secretary had been too long in government to be troubled by minor and uncheckable untruth. The President had said to the Secretary: "These things always seem to come to us as a surprise." The Secretary had passed the implied criticism along to Campbell. It might have gone to the director of the CIA who had been in attendance early in the evening. But it evidently did not occur to the amiable retired advertising executive currently heading the Agency that he was in any way involved. He had turned with interest to see how Worth Campbell responded.

"I think it's fair to say, Mr. President, that we recognized this was a weak spot before the trouble began last week. Martínez has had trouble before, but this seemed to merit closer watching. But Puerto Santos hasn't been much of an intelligence target, and it wasn't until yesterday that our people there began to feel there was immediate danger." This answer had done less than justice to O'Donnell's estimate volunteered at a Bureau staff meeting a full five days earlier. "The old fart is really on the skids this time." And his suggestion that Puerto Santos was not an intelligence target gave insufficient credit to the arrangements which, in one of the oldest traditions of the Foreign Service, O'Donnell had made with Joe Hurd by which Hurd kept O'Donnell informed by means of the regular mails. For most purposes these are sufficiently fast, and truth need not be accommodated to official preference — in this case, that of Ambassador Pethwick. Worth Campbell had assumed some such communication lay behind the O'Donnell assurance, but to mention such irregularity is, in some measure, to sanction it. Like most experienced administrators, he believed in keeping things in channels.

"I do not entirely understand the reference to a new contingency plan." This again was from Symes Jones.

"The Air Force came up with a piece of paper after our meeting this afternoon saying that if the Communists looked like taking over, the roads and supply routes used by the insurgents would be interdicted by air attack. The Joint Chiefs provisionally concurred. It was agreed that the plan should be revised."

"The Air Force couldn't have been serious," said O'Donnell. "Good Lord, can they tell a revolutionary from the air?"

"The Air Force has been restudying its role in counter-insurgency operations," the Assistant Secretary replied a trifle stiffly. "It concedes that bombing has adverse effects. Most of them agree with the Rostow doctrine that it has to be combined with a strong effort to win the minds and hearts of the people." The Assistant Secretary's lips snapped shut. It was not an argument to be prolonged at this hour.

In a moment he proceeded in a more equable tone: "Well, let's get this program off to Pethwick. When Martínez learns something is coming, he will probably give him a pretty early appointment. The Secretary initialed the White House paper. Someone can clear the telegram in the morning."

In less than an hour the telegram to Pethwick conveying the day's work had been typed, checked against the White House paper, a sentence clarified here, a word there, a few prepositions removed, "so as not," in the language of a bimonthly reminder, "to unnecessarily burden our system of communications," and it had been retyped, initialed by the three officers and sent on its way to the Communications Center along with the letter from the President of the United States to the President of Puerto de los Santos. At ten minutes after twelve, after many hours of urgent activity, the Assistant Secretary's suite of offices was dark and silent. Flores time in summer is one hour behind Washington's.

Intermezzo I

"EXCELLENCY. A word with you urgently, please."

The voice, which followed a sharp rap, came through the door of María's room. The President looked at María; she was asleep, breathing audibly. She drank a bit heavily now — but she was a good woman and loyal. It helped that she was with him at this moment. The President slipped on his shoes and reached for his tunic.

"Excellency! Excellency . . ."

There was urgency and just a trace of impatience in General Pérez's gravelly voice. The President hooked his fingers in the collar of his tunic and walked to the other room, by the dinner table with its disarray of napkins, dishes, bottles, and opened the door.

"Excellency, I fear there is little time to lose. They are coming for you at any minute."

"What about the soldiers?"

"There has been a truce. That is why the firing stopped an hour ago. It was part of the bargain, I fear, that your whereabouts would be made known."

The President did not respond. Somewhere in the deeper recesses of his mind he had realized that this moment was coming. It seemed less bad now that it was here.

"I will go to the Argentine's."

"Excellency, that is out of the question. You cannot risk an automobile. The only chance is the Embassy of Paraguay. We go out into the back alley and into their little garden."

"He is a pig."

"Yes. It cannot be helped."

The President pulled on his tunic. "I think, Excellency, that the uniform might be unwise. You have money?"

"Yes, I have money."

The two men, both stout and aging, passed down through empty rooms. The colonel's desk was deserted, a half-smoked cigar on the edge. The aide was gone. They went out through the kitchen, out into the garden and through a small gate that led into a dusty lane. A small animal scurried out of their way. The guards who should have been on duty were nowhere to be seen. A moment later the two men had let themselves into the garden of a small house, its peeling walls and decrepit aspect apparent even in the dim light. A switch clicked inside in response to their knock.

"Excellency, I shall not accompany you further, if you do not mind. My duty lies with my country. Moreover, it will be crowded, I believe. There has been a considerable movement to the embassies today. I am told the Paraguayan has only one bed." .

The door opened. Once, in imitation, the President had tried to popularize reference to the Era of Martínez. The country was too small, and the phrase was too pompous. It had not caught on except among extreme sycophants. But whatever it would be called it was now at an end — at forty-four minutes past ten. But the former President's mind was elsewhere. He had been reminded by the mention of the bed that he should have told the faithful María that he was leaving.

•

From the dark tropical sky the light of the half-moon, now high, filtered down through the palms into the streets of Flores. It was all the light there was. The street lamps, yellow, flickering and at best unreliable, were off. There was no light from the houses. A long black automobile made its way carefully down from the hill above the city. It crossed the great encircling road and continued into the streets of the old city. Once or twice, the tires crunched on broken glass. Once, it swerved to avoid an overturned car. Once, the headlights picked out two men, crouching, running rapidly into a narrow side-street. Once, the lights showed a crumpled bundle on the sidewalk below an ancient wall. It might have been some discarded clothes, some washing hurriedly dropped, and the car did not stop. It was a casualty of the revolution, a twelve-year-old boy. The car turned into a wider street leading to the palace square.

Inside the car the silhouette of the driver low behind the wheel was visible. So, dimly, was the figure sitting erect in the rear seat — black solid hat, full face, chin firmly forward. The car continued on through the silent, littered streets. Pennons flew from each fender. Pethwick was passing.

Intermezzo II

IN FLORES THAT NIGHT, apart from some bands of young-sters roaming the streets in search of further excitement, only the Club of the Saints was an island of life. In Washington the White House was dark and silent. A single guard nodded at the main door of the State Department. Beside him was a book that recorded the late departures. There was now an increasing elapse of time between entries. Here and there through the building, charwomen had turned on lights and were pursuing their cleaning machines down echoing halls and through deserted rooms. Except for one island here, all had gone.

This oasis was the Communications Center of the Department of State. It was in full operation under hard bright lights. The messages which would be the next day's business and which told of the prospects for war and peace, the progress of liberty, the dangers of subversion, the record of economic advance and retrogression, the need for decisions, and which pleaded for travel authorization, leaves of absence, new furniture and relief from unwanted visitors were pouring in from American outposts in every quarter of the globe. The men who man this center, and its varied and clattering equipment, are by no means indifferent to the weighty and sometimes appalling importance of the words that pass through their hands. If and when the world faces Armageddon they will have reflected on its implications some moments before anyone else. But beyond noticing that its priority classification would require that the duty officer advise Assistant Secretary Grant Worthing Campbell of its arrival and that it be sent out to him at his house by safe hand, a telegram coming in at this moment from Flores, Puerto Santos, aroused little interest among these admirably but most confidentially informed citizens. Pethwick's messages are in cipher and must be decoded. But there is an even more subtle art in sensing the meaning that a Pethwick message conveys.

SECRET

Flores, P. S.

Emergency Limit Distribution

SEC STATE
WASHINGTON

NOW ESTIMATE MARKED FURTHER DETERIORATION POSITION HERE. AT BEST SITUATION VERY UNCLEAR. CALLED ON MARTINEZ IN ACCORDANCE FIRM APPOINTMENT TWENTY-THREE HUNDRED HOURS LOCAL TIME TONIGHT TO ADVISE HIM HIS SECURITY NEEDS RECEIVING URGENT ATTENTION. HE DID NOT REPEAT DID NOT KEEP APPOINTMENT. REGULAR STAFF NOT ON DUTY AND IN FACE OF CONSIDERABLE CONFUSION AT PALACE UNABLE TO GET

CLEAR PICTURE OF PRESIDENT'S WHEREABOUTS OR REASON FAILURE TO KEEP WELL UNDERSTOOD APPOINTMENT. ON RETURN RESIDENCE CAR SURROUNDED BY YOUNG HOODLUMS WHO REMOVED AMBASSADOR'S FLAG, THREW STONES, VEGETABLES, BEAT ON CAR WITH BEER CANS, BOTTLES. NO POLICE IN EVIDENCE. SOME SOLDIERS IN MOB. DAMAGE TO FINISH, TRIM, ALSO TOP. BELIEVE REPAIRS FEASIBLE AND CAN BE ACCOMPLISHED HERE. INTEND PROTESTING IN STRONGEST TERMS EARLIEST TOMORROW. ABSENCE OF FIRING SINCE LATE EVENING MAY MEAN LOYAL FORCES HAVE REASSERTED CONTROL. HOWEVER FURTHER ADVERSE DEVELOPMENTS CANNOT BE RULED OUT. BELIEVE OUTRAGE MENTIONED INDICATES INSECURITY EMPHASIZING URGENT NEED PROGRAM STRONGLY SUPPORTING MARTINEZ EARLIEST POSSIBLE MOMENT. REMAINING IN CLOSEST TOUCH.

PETHWICK

7

JOHN F. KENNEDY, when President, observed that while success in the conduct of the public business has a proud parentage, failure is pretty much an orphan. That does not mean that like the classical orphans of Charles Dickens it is ignored. The fall of Martínez was not an outstanding success for American foreign policy, but, as the news spread through Washington next day, it was by no means neglected. It came up at the noon briefing of the press by William Henry McWilliams, Jr., the press officer of the Department of State — officially the Director: Office of News. The following is not the official transcript but what was actually said.

"Bill, what's the story on Martínez?"

"The Department has been in close touch with that situation for some time. It has, of course, been aware that the Martínez Administration has been under attack from certain elements in that country."

"What about this fellow Miró?"

"I cannot make any comment at this time."

"Can you give us anything off the record?"

"I think I can say strictly off the record that we have always had some concern about some of the people who appear to be back of Miró."

"Bill, does that have to be 'off the record'? Couldn't it be 'not for attribution'? God knows we're not getting much on this."

"Well, okay, I guess. Not to a 'high State Department source,' just 'some State Department sources.'"

"Was there a meeting on this at the White House this morning?"

"Anything on that would have to come from over there."

"Was it to discuss what we do down there?"

"I have no comment. You can draw your own conclusions on what was discussed."

"Sir, is it true that there was a big session at the White House only last night to consider more support for Martínez?"

"There was, I believe, a meeting to review the general situation. I can't say anything more."

"Will we recognize the Miró government?"

"I can't comment on that."

"Will what's-his-name Pethwick be recalled?"

"Ambassador Pethwick is returning to Washington for consultation."

"Is it true that he reported that Martínez could easily weather this storm?"

"I believe that he was keeping in very close touch with the situation. Beyond that I cannot comment."

"In other words, it caught him by surprise."

"I told you I *had* no comment."

"For Christ's sake, I was only asking!"

"Do we know what happened to Martínez?"

"We are informed that he has been given asylum in the Argentine Embassy in Flores."

"Sir, did I understand you to say that we would or would not recognize Miró?"

"I said I had no comment."

"Is there a character named Aragón back of Miró? It was in some paper yesterday."

"That is our information, but I have no comment."

"Bill, there is something on the wire about a guy called Obregón also getting the heave. Who is this Obregón?"

"I have no comment. I don't know about Obregón."

"Thank you, Bill. . . . Thank you, Mr. McWilliams. . . . Thank you, Bill."

•

At almost the same time, there was a discussion in the office of the Deputy Under Secretary of State for Administration. It was between the Under Secretary and the Director General of the Foreign Service who had dropped by.

"I hear they are calling Pethwick back." It was the Director General who spoke.

"Yes," said the Under Secretary for Administration. "I don't suppose he will be returning to Puerto Santos. They don't usually."

"I'd say he blotted his copybook a bit on this one. He was reporting up until midnight last night that Martínez could ride it out."

"Well," said the Under Secretary, "it isn't the first time he has made that mistake — he stuck with Syngman Rhee until the old man had been two weeks in Hawaii. And he was so close to the Prime Minister that got assassinated in Burma they nearly cremated him too. We'll have to stand back of him."

"Isn't that going a little far, Mr. Secretary? He could put in for retirement. Teach in a college somewhere."

"Look, if we don't give Pethwick another embassy we will be publicly admitting that the whole Department made a wrong guess. We can't do that."

"Yeah. But won't the President stick on giving him another job?"

"He might at first but it's his government too, remember that. There was a meeting at the White House exactly last night to consider how to back up Martínez. We were all ready to offer him the Marines, I hear."

"What about the Senate?"

"Fulbright will give Pethwick some trouble, but Ambassador Pethwick isn't any mine of information. They get tired sooner or later."

"Any thoughts on where he might go?"

"There's plenty of time for that," said the Under Secretary. After a moment's thought, he added, "Probably not Formosa."

"Schlesinger says that the Foreign Service is the only place where you get promoted for your mistakes."

"I like to think that we are not being guided in these matters by our friend Arthur."

·

There were also meetings in the office of Assistant Secretary Grant Worthing Campbell. There were several that day but only two that affected, however slightly, the course of history. The first was with William O'Donnell and the Ambassador to the Organization of American States. The Ambassador was not a man of great importance. His long political and public career was behind him. This career and his years and modest wealth entitled him to a certain consideration. But he had always shown an inclination to the premature position. Before they had become popular or even commonplace, he had been for the CIO, migrant workers, social security, the TVA, modern painting, birth control, Guy Tugwell, Harry Hopkins, Averell Harriman, Herbert Lehman, Fiorello La Guardia, Norman Thomas, Luis Muñoz Marín, José Figueres and Negro rights. Even when they were still considered dangerous, he had not denounced Marshal Tito or Nikita Khrushchev. Now in advancing years he still showed an aversion to the settled view. His manner was also against him; he had never overcome a tendency simply to blurt things out. Often what he blurted had a superficial logic that was not easily refuted. In consequence, he made Worth Campbell a trifle nervous. Also, as Campbell had long ago learned in diplomacy, nothing is more important than continuity of policy. The world is filled with men who are skillfully biding their time in order to make capital out of American mistakes. Accordingly, it is often better to continue error than to draw attention to it by changing course, and it follows that diplomacy is best practiced by people who have a resistance to novelty and no undue flexibility of mind. The Ambassador had, if anything, a predisposition to change. If a policy seemed wrong he would propose revision regardless of consequences. Finally, in diplomacy, there is always advantage in having information your opponent does not possess. So one must always keep some knowledge in reserve — play one's cards close to the chest. The Ambassador spoke his mind. In consequence, he could not be trusted with really vital matters. His approach now was all too characteristic.

"I think we should recognize Miró as soon as we can. Getting rid of Martínez was the best thing that ever happened. He never did any good to anyone except himself and maybe a few hundred women. I imagine Miró has made some kind of deal with the army down there, and without our help it probably won't last." When the Ambassador had finished he obviously didn't have much left to say.

The Assistant Secretary leaned back in his chair and locked his fingers together. The light gleamed on his rimless glasses. "I think you are right on the deal and that he may have trouble lasting without our help. I believe it was a wise decision this morning to hold off on the troops and planes — in spite of all the pressures and the risk. Their army is intact. It won't tolerate a Communist takeover so we can afford to wait. But I don't think we should rush in to help Miró out. We'd better see what he's like."

The Ambassador allowed himself one more comment. "I know something about that boy's family and background, and I believe him when he said in his manifesto that he wants to be friendly to the United States."

Again the Assistant Secretary seemed to agree. "I didn't make myself altogether clear. Apart from what Martínez has been saying, there is no direct evidence that he is a Communist, and we can discount Martínez somewhat. But we also know how skillful the Communists are at using their friends. Have you seen this?" He shoved a sheet of punched yellow paper over to the Ambassador; the latter lifted his chin to peer through the lower half of his bifocals.

Biographical Details

JOSÉ MARÍA MIRÓ-SÁNCHEZ

Strictly Confidential

Subject was born in small town of Buena Vista, Puerto Santos, May 16, 1932. Son of well-to-do farmer, rancher. Father's name Roberto M. Miró. Mother's name Sánchez. Educated Catholic (Jesuit) school, Flores, Academia Militar de la República (State Military Academy). No known college association radical elements. Commissioned in Puerto Santos army. Became active in young officers' group identified hostile to regime. Discharged or resigned from army, date unclear. Left country, traveled in Venezuela, Costa Rica. Trip to Cuba possible at this time. Attended University of Puerto Rico one year. Believed in close touch this period other dissident elements including socialists, Catholics, former army personnel, liberals, political *émigrés*, Communists, including Castroites. Disaffection said to be related expropriation father by Martínez government. At some stage, date unclear, returned Puerto Santos, joining anti-Martínez underground, later assumed leadership of dissident movement. Numerous warrants for arrest. Said by official sources to be ambitious, expedient, willing to work with any and all opponents of established government. Proclaims willingness to use violence to get rid of Martínez. Martínez frequently describes him as Communist. Believed to have associations with (first name uncertain) Aragón, identified Communist agent. Has put out comprehensive political program including land reform, elections, economic development, free education, friendship all nations, higher prices sugar and coffee, full employment, public water supplies, sewage disposal, housing, urban redevelopment, peace, educational television. Materials correcting, amending or supplementing this biography should be sent for evaluation and possible use to Room 2306 A, Central Intelligence Agency, Langley, Virginia.

The Ambassador passed the paper to O'Donnell who passed it back to the Assistant Secretary. "I've seen it; in fact, I gave them some of it," he said. "As a reason for not recognizing Miró it's a lot of balls."

The Assistant Secretary's face tinged ever so slightly. "No," he replied very evenly, "I don't think it is a lot of balls. And even if it were we would have to be very, very sure." Turning to the Ambassador he said yet more evenly, "I think you realize what it would mean to be wrong — to support a Communist down there and what it would mean to those who made the mistake, the Administration, that is?" It is possible that at this moment Worth Campbell's position on Miró, as the State Department would say, hardened. If so, some of the responsibility lay with Bill O'Donnell.

There was little more of importance. The Ambassador asked the Assistant Secretary if he saw any alternative to Miró. The Assistant Secretary replied that in his experience with Latin America there were always plenty of alternatives. He omitted, as when speaking of Martínez, to confess his unfamiliarity with their names.

·

The second conference was with an important journalist, a man who disdained that term and spoke of himself as a reporter. In his columns he says "This reporter." In China, Santo Domingo, Panama, Guatemala, Brazil, Indonesia, Guinea, Ghana, Burma, South Vietnam, Macao, Hong Kong, the Philippines, Berkeley, the Congo, Laos and the liberal wing of the Vatican, he has disclosed the work of the Communists. In all except the last he has, at one time or another, predicted a Communist take-over. He was right about China, and, possibly, his warnings have prevented this disaster in the other places. The misfortune of the man who predicts doom is that he may set in motion the steps that prevent it. Thus he saves mankind at the price of his reputation as a prophet. Notwithstanding this handicap, this reporter is a cause of public anxiety in an average of one hundred and forty-seven papers every day.

"How close are they to moving in?" The pronoun needed no antecedents. The two spoke the common shorthand of the veterans of this war.

"We simply do not know. Some of the people back of Miró look pretty bad."

"Moscow, Mao or Castro?"

"We don't know. Probably some of all."

"Miró is a front, then?"

"More likely an instrument. Maybe quite decent and honest. We know how the Communists can use that kind of man."

"What does the Agency say, Mr. Secretary?" The reporter had long ago learned that you never got information in Washington by pretending to a false familiarity. Far better accord the man the dignity which makes him feel that he has the right to be a source of news.

"Pretty much what I have just told you. Until a few days ago they didn't have any operation to speak of down there. You can't spy everywhere, it seems. That's strictly off the record, of course."

"Of course. So we may be in line for a take-over."

"I am not predicting anything," said the Assistant Secretary, and then, putting a shade of emphasis on each word, he added, "but we have a dangerous situation, and we can't run any risks in that part of the world. We simply can't run any risks at all."

"What could we put in if we had to?"

"No problem. The Air Force is ready to bomb, although we would have to face the usual liberal and world reaction. A Marine division would be easy — hopefully as part of an OAS force. But maybe we can just wait; running that country is no picnic, money will be scarce, and the army is intact. Our estimate is that it will not stand for too much Communist nonsense. Our worst problem will be here at home — people who will want to play along with Miró and with his backers and who could save them."

"Pretty soft-minded."

"Very soft-minded, but we've always had them. And I sometimes think there are more of them every year."

"Well, I don't think the American people will stand for another Cuba."

"I have been making that point all day," said the Assistant Secretary.

"Maybe I can just give you a little help."

The great reporter made his way out, down the hall, down the elevator and to his waiting chauffeur and car. As he drove away there was a glint in his eye.

·

The American press, it has often been said by thoughtful journalists themselves, plays a vital role in the government of a democracy. In support of this role, at least two other officials talked that day with members of what is called, sometimes a trifle ambiguously, the working press. One was Bill O'Donnell. His communication was with a reporter who was leaving next morning for Flores. In normal times no full-time member of the American press is resident in that capital. The wire services rely on local men for routine stories on nominations, elections and inaugurations, matters in which, over the last thirty years, there has been a very small element of surprise, and also for news of government crisis of which, in this period, there has been none, and for news of the occasional hurricane and airplane crash in which, since the people suffering have always been unknown and often poor, the interest in the world at large has been far from keen. Plots against the regime, and resulting arrests, torture, mysterious disappearance or exile, although of undoubted interest to the people of Puerto Santos, were not regarded locally as legitimate news. They were circulated only by word of mouth. This worked surprisingly well within the country, but it produced no hard information that could be put on the wires to Washington or New York.

When word that the Martínez regime was in trouble had seeped out the wire services, the Washington *Post* and the *New York Times* had each dispatched a man of modest competence to Flores. This advance guard had been in residence for several days. Now, as the news of the fall of Martínez spread through Washington the fire brigade, which stands ready to fly to what its more eloquent members refer to as the Newsfronts of the World, began to move, as one man, on Friendship and Dulles. The big resort hotel on the hill near Flores faced demands on its moldering resources that it had not experienced since the days of the first wedding of the oldest daughter of Luis Miguel Martínez Obregón to a minor Moroccan prince whose tendencies were so outrageous that eventually she rather tired of them. The prospect for the Flores telegraph office was equally appalling. Fortunately, as so often happens with the Washington fire brigade, it would arrive after the worst was over.

Bill O'Donnell's information was given over the telephone in response to an incoming call. Although he disliked to think of himself as a cautious man, and although there is no rule against State Department officials talking to reporters, his telephone manner was restrained, even circumspect.

"Joe Hurd will be Chargé. He is a good man, well-informed and has political sense which you can't say for his former boss, the Ambassador. Joe should be very helpful. I happen to know for he has been my source down there. Give him my highly classified regards. The poor bastard has had a hard time in the last couple of years and has a bleeding ulcer. The good men get ulcers in this Christ-bitten profession, but the boneheads are very healthy. Joe doesn't think Miró is a Communist. That means that his reports will be read here with reserve if you follow our careful habits of speech. Make up your own mind if that is allowed in your line of business . . . Not at all. I wish I was going with you . . . 'Bye."

•

The other communication was between a Brigadier General of the Joint Staff of the Joint Chiefs of Staff of the Department of Defense on assignment as assistant to the Special Assistant for Counter Insurgency and Special Activities and an editor of the weekly journal that more Americans in the higher buying-power range rely on than any other for a concise and authoritative report on what lies just ahead in the nation's capital. Communication by the general with the editor was strictly illegal; officers on duty in the Department of Defense are required regularly to read and initial a circular which tells of the desire of the Department to avoid anything that "smacks of censorship" but warns of "the chaos that could only result if members of the armed services were to freely talk on pending policy and security questions to the representatives of the press." The general almost invariably obeyed orders. However, he did have friends in the press, and he was less worried about chaos than most. A follower of the major intellectual currents of the time, he had once heard a leading savant from the University of Chicago expound on its merits. In contrast with planning, chaos was highly favorable to free enterprise. And it was not spot news that he was releasing, only a guide to dangers imperfectly appreciated by the American people and to which as a patriot he wished to see them alerted. Here, in due course, is what appeared:

> Hottest cold war trouble spot now on the horizon is Puerto Santos, U.S. military men now say. Communists are mobilizing strongly behind José Miró who in a showdown is expected to do their bidding. Word is that another Cuba is in the making. Count on firm action.

History is not made exclusively in capitals. While news of the fall of Martínez fell on Washington with primary impact, there were other places on which it made a strong impression. It was heard in New York by the Puerto Santos *émigrés* and, in the main, with unalloyed pleasure. Some thought of returning to Flores and dismissed the thought. The sacrifice would be excessive. That is why *émigré* movements in the United States quickly diminish to a few elderly functionaries who seek to offset with indignation the apathy of those far more numerous compatriots for whom American exile has meant better jobs at better pay than they ever dreamed possible. Some thought of getting their property back. In the main, they, too, dismissed the thought. They knew that, however reluctantly, they had signed valid contracts of sale, and in the end were glad to go.

The news was also heard though with less pleasure at the Consulates-General of the Republic of Puerto de los Santos in New York, Miami, Las Vegas, Los Angeles and New Orleans in which restful precincts various relatives, friends and enemies, whom the dictator had allowed or encouraged to live outside of the country, wondered if they would have now to work for a living and whether anything hitherto so unimaginable would be tolerable.

The news was also heard in Ann Arbor, Michigan, where Juan César Martínez picked it up on the radio as he was about to leave for a class in Social Aspects of Economic Development. He continued on to class. At noon he had lunch by himself at one of the small restaurants off the campus and thought about the news and then went to a seminar on research methods at the Survey Research Center. During the seminar he thought more about his father's fall, but not as much as might be imagined for, in a way, he too had long been expecting it. He guessed that one or two of the participants glanced at him with curiosity, but he couldn't be sure. He had learned long since that he aroused very little interest. Once a returned Rhodes scholar had told of a Prince of the Imperial House of Japan who was making his initial appearance as a student at Magdalen College, Oxford. The occasion called for a special greeting by the President of the College, a properly proud man, who inquired of the Prince as to his formal title. The latter replied that in his own country he was known as the Son of Heaven. "You will find many other famous people here," the President had observed reassuringly. It was much the same at the University of Michigan. The editor of the *Daily*, the members of the football team, the leading campus revolutionaries, two or three admitted geniuses, the son of a senior vice-president of General Motors, a member of a cadet branch of the Fords, and several articulate defenders of drug addiction ranked well above the son of a dictator of a distant land. A girl with a good-humored, slightly plump face, intelligent eyes, nice brown hair and nondescript but encouraging figure, joined him as he left the seminar.

"I heard about your father. Do you feel very badly? I mean, should I be sorry?"

"No, he's probably all right. It had to come some day, and the radio said he was safe in the Brazilian Embassy."

"What do you mean it had to come?"

"For one thing he was getting on in years. But also he belonged to the past."

"What do you mean 'the past'? Are dictators finished?"

"His kind, I think. You wouldn't want George Romney owning the whole state and being Governor for life. Or Soapy Williams."

"Not Romney. Will you have to go home?"

"I don't think so now. A lot of people will now be taking it out on the old man — some of them with good reason. And they might make it a bit rough for the rest of us. I better wait."

"Do you have enough money to keep on here?"

"Oh, sure. More than enough. The old man took precautions. Did you ever hear of a numbered account?"

"In Zurich?"

"Ours, I believe, are in Geneva. We like the Latin touch. I imagine my oil company will soon be losing interest in me, though."

"I am glad I don't have to be sorry for you. My sympathy is never convincing."

They walked across the campus. It was hot and dry, and the leaves rustled slightly like pieces of dry paper in the slight breeze. Students in summer undress passed them; the couple, slightly short, one a little dark, both unremarkable, attracted no attention and only once received any greeting. They passed the wide stretch of the athletic fields, now brownish-green except where the sprinklers had been on, and turned down a side-street toward the apartment.

"Come up for a while?" It was a question rather than an invitation.

"Are your intentions honorable?"

"I have to be faithful to my culture."

"That's nice. I like faithful men. I was reading in some article that your father was very faithful too."

"They exaggerate a little but not much. He was supposed, in his prime, to have had a different woman every night — or afternoon, I guess it was."

"Goodness. How did you know who your mother was?"

"Our family situation was quite separate, I promise you that." There was a perceptible stiffness in his voice.

"I'm sorry. I shouldn't have joked about such things. Mothers, especially."

"It's all right. A man in the *New Republic* once said that my father wanted to be the father of his country and went about it in the only way he knew. I imagine he more or less succeeded."

"Are you going to the Vietnam meeting tonight?"

"I think I will have to moderate my enthusiasm for Vietnam democracy until I see what is happening to Martínez democracy. I've always been afraid that someone would make a connection between the two — and tonight I'd be asking for it."

"You greatly exaggerate the perception of our fellow democrats . . . Jesus! Sorry!"

The last exclamation came as they passed into the dark, slightly old-fashioned lobby of the apartment building. A photographer had detached himself from the fumed oak paneling and stepped forward with a flash camera to take their picture. Now a reporter materialized with a notebook. The day's involvement of Puerto Santos with a free and responsible press was not quite over.

"I wonder if you have any statement on the . . . on the discontinuation of your father's government, Mr. Martínez?"

"I'm afraid I don't."

"You are naturally disappointed, aren't you?"

"I am afraid I wouldn't want to say."

"Could you tell us when you first heard of it?"

"On the radio this morning."

"Did it come as a shock?"

"I am afraid I wouldn't like to say."

"I mean, were you expecting it?"

"No."

"Do you think your country will now go Communist?"

"No."

"Could you give us the name of this young lady?" The photographer was asking.

"No."

"If you don't, they will print that you were accompanied by an 'unidentified woman companion.'"

"I suppose that would be roughly the truth."

"Yeah. But a lot of people don't think it sounds good. They may have you at a misapprehension."

·

The young couple made their way into the elevator. Juan Martínez punched the button a little as though he meant it to hurt.

"Why couldn't I get my name in the papers too?"

"I didn't know you craved it, baby."

8

SINCE 1945, the winds of change have been blowing through Latin America. In Puerto Santos, it is generally agreed, they diminish to a rather light breeze. Nonetheless they have been felt. Students, travelers, men of business returning to Flores from New York, Washington, Mexico, even Spain, have found the country dull: no newspapers worthy of the name, no university worthy of the name, cautious speech combined with highly unimaginative praise of Martínez. In Latin America it no longer seems quite respectable to live under a dictatorship and especially the Latin American kind. One is diminished — a second-class citizen. So it has been even in Puerto Santos.

Other influences have been felt. Fifty years ago, a wealthy sugar or coffee planter had a very good life in Puerto Santos, and in New York or the south of France it was something to be a rich Latin American. And whether one was something or not it was very enjoyable. These being privileges worth fighting for, men fought for them

— and supported governments that promised to sustain them. But Martínez liquidated this elite; or, more precisely, his particular version of Marx's capitalist concentration made it coordinate with the Martínez family. And rich Latin Americans no longer have much standing in the world. There are too many others who are rich. In consequence the country has lost its most passionate defenders of privilege and those who most urgently counseled the poor to be contented with their lot.

Washington has contributed to the restlessness. Older people remember promises of a bright new future pictured by the United States during World War II when it was also important that Latin Americans provide no comfort to Adolf Hitler. Nelson Rockefeller's visits were memorable in this regard; something was doubtless owing to his almost boyish sincerity. Milton Eisenhower also raised expectations; he was, after all, the President's brother. Vice-President Nixon's visit was less remembered, because he confined himself to complimenting President Martínez on his staunch anti-Communism and praising his support to the cause of freedom, always excluding Puerto Santos. (Even in the Puerto Santos of Martínez there was some slight rowdyism during this visit not attributable to affection, but happily nothing sufficient to constitute a seventh crisis in Mr. Nixon's life.) The promises of President Kennedy of a better life for Latin Americans in general and the people of Puerto Santos in particular were taken very seriously. His brother has also been heard with attention. And even the careful speeches of Assistant Secretary of State and U.S. Coordinator of the Alliance for Progress, Grant Worthing Campbell, have not gone entirely unnoticed. He has said that he believes Latin Americans should produce more, thus earn higher wages and thus have more food, better clothing and decent schools for their children. The injunction to produce more sounds like the age-old plea of the plantation owners for harder work. But the food, clothing and schools would be welcome. Campbell insists that development must take place under "sound democratic auspices." This also is welcomed, although his insistence that Castro and the Communists are the decisive enemies of democracy seems in light of local history rather implausible in Puerto Santos. There is also some uncertainty as to what he means by "maximum reliance on the progressive forces of private enterprise." No one has encountered that sort of thing in this republic.

This desire for change is surprisingly general. Teachers in the parochial schools, an occasional priest who has responded to the new stirring in Rome, those whose work brings them in touch with tourists and visiting businessmen, bus drivers who get around and accordingly act as tutors to their colleagues in the bars at night, even ordinary workers have felt it. It is mentioned more than one imagines in the distant clusters of shacks and huts on the sugar *centrales* and the coffee *fincas*. There it often begins with the question as to why the people of some countries are so very rich and those of Puerto Santos are nearly all so very poor. For this depressing circumstance is now widely known.

.

"We have always been unlucky in this country. I suppose it is the will of God."

"Is that what your wife learns from that fat blackbird to whom she tells your sins? I suppose he teaches her that the North Americans are rich because they are the special children of God."

"No. You are right. God could not have adopted all of them. I am told even Miss Elizabeth Taylor is rich."

"Then it is because our soil is poor?"

"No, I've heard that not even the cane fields of Cuba are as fertile as ours."

"Is it that we are all lazy and all stupid?"

"No, our people work hard enough when there are jobs and the foreman is watching. And they would not be so stupid if there were schools."

"Then what is the reason we are poor?"

"You have told me often. It is the thieves that run the government and own the land. They think only of themselves. But what does one do?"

•

Perhaps more surprisingly, this hope of change has penetrated the army. Among the younger officers are a number who no longer regard army service as a lifetime sinecure or the natural path to political preferment and graft. Rather, in a still hazy and incoherent way, they believe the armed forces should be a force for the modernization of Puerto Santos. Those who feel this way are a minority, and it may well be that theirs is an illusion of youth that will pass. Still, if you go through the officers' quarters you will encounter pictures of President Kennedy. And, regrettably, were you to go through the foot-lockers you would uncover an occasional picture of Fidel Castro.

For in Puerto Santos there is no absolute unanimity that the United States is the best model to follow. There are numerous and divergent opinions.

"The only solution is a revolution. Mexico is prosperous because they got rid of the dictators and landlords and the idle priests. People there have something to work for."

"What about Cuba?"

"Who can say? Maybe things will one day be better there too."

"But the Americans won't stand for a revolution in this country."

"Cuba and Mexico are the closest to the United States. Only they have had great revolutions. It must have been because they are so close."

"You are not serious?"

"I am a dumb soldier, but some things I can see. People in Mexico and Cuba could look at the United States and see that something was wrong. Our misfortune is to be too far away."

"Maybe the North Americans secretly encouraged the revolutions in Mexico and Cuba. They do not like poverty such as ours right on their doorstep."

"It is only logical. Still it may not be true."

•

In more advanced discussion it is said that while Puerto Santos and the United States have had a close if involuntary association for a hundred years, it is one that has worked rather better for the United States than for Puerto Santos. And it is being said that while North Americans outdo even Latin Americans on promises, they do not sufficiently outdo them on performance. The effect of the latter on the average man has so far been nonexistent. For though, perhaps happily, statistics to prove the point are absent, the people of Puerto Santos are almost certainly poorer now than in the days of Spain. The Martínez government never recognized the government of Red China. Nor the Union of Soviet Socialist Republics. Nor the government of Fidel Castro. The works of Marx and Lenin and Mao Tse-tung are not read in Puerto Santos; not many can read, and the attention of those who can is captured by more appetizing literature. It must be supposed that occasional agents from the Communist lands have come through Puerto Santos. If so, they must have thought it a place of limited promise.

Yet the soil could be cultivated. Mexico and Cuba again come into the conversation. Mexico once risked American anger and is now the most progressive of Latin American states. On all occasions of public ceremony it is so described by American Presidents. Cuba more recently risked American wrath. Doubtless she will one day be praised. Perhaps, it is said, Puerto Santos should also try, through revolution, to earn the future plaudits of American Presidents.

To Grant Worthing Campbell this is hideous error based on frightful illusion. Yet his experience, though it has been much enriched by the great men with whom he has served, has its own gaps. He has not lived on the *centrales* or in the *barrios* or even in the better residential districts of Flores. Great men, as he has known them, are not an impeccable guide to social thought in these precincts.

•

It was out of the various forces stirred by these vagrant gusts that José María Miró, Provisional President of the new revolutionary government of Puerto Santos, had now to fashion the support for his new administration. But his problem was more serious than that. The truce that brought an end to the fighting an hour or two before the old dictator made his way to the Paraguayan Embassy was based, as the informed suspected, on a compromise. Not loyalty to principle, not fealty to persons, but something very close to shared greed lay behind this arrangement. This is not wholly to be regretted; more often than is imagined it is what makes government possible. Miró had promised the Martínez generals that he would respect their pay and perquisites, continue them in their commissions and show good faith by giving them some of the key jobs in his new administration. Their alternative was to string along with the decaying Martínez regime to an unknown end.

Some Martínez henchmen had feared that, with the best of intentions, Miró could not prevent a measure of popular retribution when the jail doors were flung open. After nearly two centuries the shadow of the Bastille and the Paris mob reached with improbable length to the city of Flores. Thus the diaspora to the other Latin American embassies. But most of the military remained. So, in addition to meeting the demands of his diverse reformers, Miró had to meet the demands of the army. And it was in a position to back these up with the excellent weapons it had received over the years from the United States. The arm of American military assistance is long.

On the day following the revolution, Flores gave itself over to jubilation. Crowds surged through the capital with impromptu signs extrolling Miró and carrying at shoulder height some of the more prominent of the persons just released from jail. Occasional signs denounced the United States and Ambassador Pethwick. Jaime Martínez had meant to take refuge in an embassy but had gone into a whorehouse by mistake or possibly as a matter of habit. He was as usual very drunk. When extracted he was taken through the streets with only his head and large torso protruding from the orifice at the back of a municipal garbage truck. It is doubtful that he knew what was happening, although not even Jaime could have thought it a gesture of approval. But mostly the crowd was good-natured. Repeatedly it coalesced on the square in front of the white marble palace and called for Miró; repeatedly he came out on a balcony to wave and make a brief speech that could not be heard. Thereafter, his hand slightly strengthened, he went back to a small and stifling room — the electricity, and hence the air-conditioning, was still off — to wrangle with his supporters and the generals over the distribution of jobs. Toward evening the new cabinet was announced. There was considerable letdown when it was learned that General Pérez Castillo would be the new Minister of National Defense. The generals had also been given the Ministry of Public Works, long esteemed as a source of graft which, through various shadowy kickbacks from American entrepreneurs, also allowed a sizable commission on American aid. They also got the Ministry of Public Recreation, the Ministry of Public Transport, the Ministry of Public Morals and Religion and two or three sinecures. By fighting hard, Miró was able to save the Ministry of the Interior with its control of the police and the courts for the ablest and most articulate of his own friends, Luis Carlos Madera. Aged thirty, a member of an old Puerto Santos family which had salvaged some of its money, graduate of Yale and the London School of Economics, traveler, socialist, accomplished writer and, unfortunately, rather heavy drinker, Carlos Madera was not, as many alleged, constitutionally anti-American. But he could be critical, and on one memorable occasion on a television panel in New York on Latin American policy, Ambassador Pethwick had been cited in defense of President Martínez. Madera had dismissed him, untactfully, as a man who in a more heroic age would have been a Fascist but was now only a fool. Later he had hazarded the guess that most Cubans liked Castro at least as well as Batista. The Pethwicks are from Peoria, Illinois, where the family is on good terms with Everett McKinley Dirksen. The Senator's defense of Pethwick naturally gained Madera considerable publicity. Miró considered himself fortunate in getting him in charge of the police. He could be counted upon to move with vigor born of indignation to reverse the methods of the old regime.

In the bars and along the streets that night, there was much shaking of heads over the reappearance of General Pérez.

"It is the same old crowd, señor. I tell you that this fellow Miró is like all the rest. Whatever happens, the politicians and the generals look after themselves and we get kicked in the ass."

But the appointment of Madera helped: "Things will, I think, be better. This man Madera is honest and speaks his mind. He will keep those ruffians in the white helmets a little in hand."

There was another interesting appointment. Roberto Ryan was of a family also long in Puerto Santos although never of the wealth of the Mirós or the Maderas. Since the first Ryan had come ashore a century ago as a reformed soldier of fortune and before that a refugee from the great hunger, one had been a dock foreman in Santos, one had been a coffee shipper on a small scale, several had been common laborers, one had had a small farm and a very large family near Flores, half a dozen had been politicians of no significance, one, a distinguished physician, rose to be rector of the University of Puerto Santos and four had been priests. In keeping with this diversity of family background, Roberto Ryan, a grandson of the small farmer near Flores, was generally believed to be a Communist. As such he was linked in the more informed public mind with a shadowy character named Aragón who had once lived for a number of years in Puerto Santos.

Exiled (as were Ryan, Madera and Miró) by Martínez, he had long traveled through Central and South America on behalf of obscure and dubious causes. Strikes and disorder erupted in his wake. Ryan's association with Aragón did not commend itself to Miró. But Ryan appealed to Miró's younger supporters. They liked his outspoken criticism of the United States and his support for socialization of the sugar *centrales*. With Ryan in office there was some chance that those who shared his views and his nuisance value would be reasonably content and somewhat quiet. With Ryan out of office they would surely make trouble, for Ryan would organize it. Miró made Ryan Minister of Education. The title is formidable; education is something that Communists are known to take seriously. And the practical power of the post in the absence of an educational system is not great.

.

The appointment to the jobs and the festivities in the streets consumed the first day of the Miró Administration. That evening, eager to assess the portent of this revolution for the free world, the American press arrived by Pan Am jet in force. The excitement was by then over. There was some merriment in the streets until midnight, but many people were tired. On the following morning everyone went back either to work or to what, in the absence of occupation, is used to consume the hot and languorous hours in Puerto Santos. During the afternoon, President Miró had his first conference with his Finance Minister.

Personal loyalty together with an instinct to conservatism — the feeling that money must always be treated with the solemnity that goes with age and careful tailoring — had governed this appointment. Also, the generals were deeply uninterested. Miró had brought back into public life the only man in Puerto Santos who was in the slightest degree known to the world financial community. Sr. Andrés Medina Alvarez had been for many years the head of the Flores branch of the Royal Bank of Canada. For a period after World War II, when Martínez was seeking international respectability and also some loans in New York, he was head of the central bank of the Republic, the Bank of Puerto de los Santos. In this capacity he attended meetings of the World Bank and the International Monetary Fund and negotiated a loan with the Export-Import Bank in Washington. He had once published an article in *Foreign Affairs* on the prospect for a Latin American common market. It had been written by an enthusiastic young man from Salt Lake City who had worked temporarily for the Bank on an exchange arrangement with the Federal Reserve. But Sr. Medina had never got along well with Martínez and, eventually, he had been eased out, in fact fired. He lost some of his real estate but had continued to live comfortably in Flores on his Canadian bank pension and under the protection of his North American financial connections. He was still erect at seventy, with pink skin and sparkling white hair. He always wore the careful, well-pressed, more than slightly uncomfortable uniform of his former profession. He was the friend Joe Hurd had visited. It was he, with his friend in rumpled white, who had occupied and held the Santos

Club pending the arrival of Miró on the night but one earlier. Thereafter he had slept well. He now spoke:

"There seems, on hurried examination, to be no money at all."

"What do you mean?"

"Just that. The accounts to the extent that they exist are in considerable disorder. A general reorganization accompanied by a thoroughgoing audit is clearly called for. But so far as can be determined from those who should know, the Republic is devoid of funds. I might add, as a somewhat experienced observer, that this does not come to me wholly as a surprise."

"Aren't there taxes coming in?"

"Tax revenues," said the Minister, speaking a little sententiously, "have never flowed into the Puerto Santos treasury in great volume. I expect that as Martínez acquired revenue-producing property, he improved on his personal economic situation by omitting to pay taxes. That would be natural. As a student of political economy, I do not believe I ever encountered the case of a man paying taxes that he had levied on himself."

"Why can't we seize Martínez's property, bank accounts and the rest?"

"That would reflect a certain measure of retributive justice, since he stole them in the first place. I could not oppose this action. But, alas, the liquid assets precisely because they are liquid will have flowed elsewhere. And those that are not liquid cannot be used to pay salaries and other bills. One cannot use a coffee *finca* to pay the salary of your good General Pérez."

"If it were big enough, I don't expect he would mind, the old thief. I don't suppose we can borrow money?"

"My old bank would not consider the credit of the Republic adequate at this time. Nor would any other financial institution of minimum competence. Many would not consider its credit to exist. We are prevented from borrowing any more money from the Bank of Puerto Santos by agreement with the International Monetary Fund."

"What does that mean?"

"I have no idea. And I am now of an age where I do not need to pretend to knowledge that I do not possess."

"I must say that you're not very helpful. Could I perhaps remind you that you are now the Finance Minister of this bloody country?"

"By your strong plea and my slightly reluctant agreement, Mr. President. But I am aware of my responsibilities. I will, as the Americans say, do some scrounging. The Post Office. The Land Bank. The Coffee Promotion Fund. The Government Pension Fund. We can only hope that Martínez overlooked some of these. We must appeal to the patriotism of the oil companies and their natural uneasiness at a time like this. The aluminum people will also be taking a thoughtful view of the future of their concession. They will surely be good for a modest loan. But, Mr. President, it cannot be much. Hardly enough to cover the payroll for a month."

"It might be smarter to pay the generals and the army for two months and let the rest starve. But what about the people? You heard them cheering yesterday. I've promised them jobs and schools and a hospital here and in Santos. And some action on the slums. Water. Sewers. Paved streets. I can't disappoint them. If I don't do these things they might just as well have Martínez again."

"In my experience, Mr. President, one can always find money in the long run. Given time we can realize something on the Martínez property. We can have taxes on exports. More on imports. In these last years it has been patriotic not to pay taxes in Puerto Santos — maybe it never was. We can make default, if not unpatriotic, at least a trifle more uncomfortable. But that is in the future. We must have money now. For that there is only one place."

"I think I can guess. The United States?"

"Mr. President, you are very right. The United States. Someone of high reliability must be dispatched there as soon as possible to smooth the way. The good Ambassador Ramírez will not do."

"Lord, no! I've already sent him a message saying he is without employment. I don't think he will want to return home."

"His selection as Ambassador to Washington was not entirely illogical," said the Minister. "For a professional procurer getting money and arms in Washington must be the top of the ladder. I imagine that, given his personal tendencies, he will not want to remain in the United States without diplomatic immunity."

"It would be unwise. I wonder where he could go . . . Saudi Arabia, maybe. Who do you suggest we send to Washington?"

9

As the President and the Finance Minister parted, the slanting sun was lighting up the salmon-pink walls of the big resort hotel on the hill above the town. It was a pleasant sight, although less pleasant where it showed the cracks in the stucco and the unpatched holes and the naked lath. The sun also lit up the bougainvillea in the hotel grounds, and it was a blaze of violent purple. It lit up the great palms with their fat and ungainly boles resembling huge pineapples. It fell on untidy banana trees around the border. And the sun reached across the coarse, sparse, uneven grass to two white Leghorn hens which were scratching industriously in one corner. The sun and shadow also fell across the derelict tennis court and the dry swimming pool with its flaking, sun-bleached paint that was once a rich sky-blue and now disappeared in its depths into the leaves, old papers, cardboard containers, bottles and derelict deck chair that covered the bottom.

Twenty-four hours had now passed since the press had

arrived in force, and they had been ones of indescribable confusion. An angry mob still besieged the desk.

"I tell you that operator has never answered."

"What about the water?"

"But I think it would be cooler on the other side."

"Look here, my man, we aren't exactly getting these rooms for nothing."

"¿Habla inglés?"

"When will the water be turned on?"

"I ordered that car first thing this morning."

"I've got deadlines, newspaper deadlines, to meet, y'understand?"

"You have no idea how it smells after three or four times."

"Could I please see the . . ."

"But it was promised for . . ."

The desk clerks and the assistant manager took it all in good part. They were experienced in handling complaints on the shortcomings of this hotel. Never previously had they had such a good excuse. "But, señor, you must realize that these are difficult times. A revolution. In Washington and New York you are naturally not accustomed . . ."

In the lobby of the hotel, strongly reminiscent of a pile of junk just culled out of an attic, stood great heaps of television equipment. Cameras, tripods, innumerable square suitcases, rolls of cable, all dull black, all shabby, all bearing the heraldry of the Columbia Broadcasting System, had been there since their arrival the evening before. The electricity being off, the elevator was not running. They were too heavy to carry upstairs. The producer and the news commentator surveyed the disaster.

"I can't understand why you didn't run the regular head count in Miami." It was the commentator who asked, and he was irritated.

"I did, and fourteen answered present. Apparently one of the sound men got confused and answered twice."

"Couldn't we go ahead and film without an assistant tripod-spotter just this once?"

"The union, my lad, the union. Artists cannot go around moving tripods, much less assisting with such menial labor."

"What about recruiting a local hand?"

"I hired a fellow this morning that the hotel recommended, when you were out casing the revolution. But when I explained about the union, he quit. He said Martínez was opposed to unions."

"But look, Martínez is gone," said the commentator. "Surely he knew that."

A couple of newspapermen stopped to eavesdrop, and the producer glanced at them and lowered his voice to a faint mutter.

"They're still not running any risks down here, I guess. Or maybe the man was a bit retarded which is too bad, for he might have done well in this business. Anyway, he spoke practically no English."

"I am reporting on radio this evening that they are expecting a full-scale Communist take-over at midnight. I got that straight from the colonel who was the personal aide to Martínez — with him to the last. How are we going to cover that?"

"It won't matter too much. I've never known a revolution to come over well on television."

·

Out in the palm lounge which fronted on the deep end of the dry swimming pool, two old hands, men whose bylines are a byword wherever there is trouble, were settling down to their ease on the wicker chairs.

"Bit of a frenzy."

"It always is, more or less. What are you drinking?"

"Rum. I believe in sticking to the wine of the country."

"I simply can't take it. Waiter, what have you got?" The waiter, who had been flicking at the flies on the tables with a very dirty rag, ranged alongside.

"Rum punch, señor. Also rum collins. Planter's punch."

"What else?"

"Some very good Bacardi rum, señor."

"All right, a rum punch. What do you make of things?"

"After years of peace and tranquillity this country now faces a sad and troubled future. Initiative is clearly with the extremists." The journalist was quoting the lead of the story he had just sent off. His companion recognized the art form and said: "Very well put. I take it you mean the left?"

"You saw the cabinet list. A strong anti-American and Castro supporter in charge of the police. A known Communist in charge of education. I was told General Pérez isn't completely trustworthy, which is probably significant.

This Aragón remains in the background which is very significant. It's a pattern. A pattern!"

"And close to the old canal. Are you going to stay around for the Marines?"

"Depends on how long. Hullo, darling! Did you get the woman's angle?"

A tall girl in a white cotton skirt, sleeveless blouse and wearing a 35-millimeter Japanese camera had come up beside one of the chairs.

"Not really; it's not even completely clear that this Miró is married. New York functioning as usual."

"All the better for you, dear. Find anyone else?"

"Yes, I saw the mistress of old Martínez. She was with him the last night. Strictly a bag but rather touching. The one great love of his life. She let me buy her some drinks."

"Did she have any news of him?"

"She says he took refuge in the American Embassy and was then taken out and scuppered by the CIA. All done out at the municipal abattoir. Corpse cut up and put through a sausage machine. The rest of the details were rather gory."

"I wouldn't go overboard on that story, honey."

"Well, then don't go using it yourself. See you." She swung her skirt and camera through a circle arc and left.

"You would think they would make a third cup for the camera."

"A good idea," said the other reporter. After a moment's thought, he added, "It would have to be smaller. Where are you eating tonight?"

"I'm dining with the Ambassador. Old friend. Covered him in Korea. Burma."

"I hear he was recalled to Washington yesterday afternoon."

The buzz in the lobby rose to a low, angry roar with occasional louder shouts. Bits of profanity drifted out. From long experience the two correspondents rose to investigate.

A spacious room off the lobby, in better days intended for bridge, had been converted into a pressroom. Three or four ancient typewriters added a professional touch, but they were not used, for almost all of the reporters had brought their own. The entire press corps was milling around the notice board to inspect and discuss a message that had just been pinned up. It was in English and read as follows:

Due to the pressure of his numerous public works, the Provisional President of the Republic, his Excellency José María Miró announces that he will not be in a position to grant any more petitions from the visiting foreign press for personal and preclusive interviews. He wishes to state that he will meet with his friends of the visiting foreign press for an interview of questions and answers tomorrow 1700 hours, 5 P.M. old style.

> E. Cervantes
> Provisional Press Officer

The two old hands waited until the struggle subsided, read the message and strolled away.

"Who do you suppose got the exclusives?"

"Someone claiming to represent one of our old and established journals. The New York *Sun, Herald Trib,* Washington *Times-Herald,* Boston *Evening Transcript.*"

"I suppose so. Maybe the *Daily Worker.*"

.

"You will see why it's hard for us to go home. I had twenty-two requests for interviews today. In twelve years in Washington I was only asked once. That was when I was elected president, *in absentia,* of the PTA of the school my kid attended in Silver Spring. I heard people thought they were voting for a real estate man by the same name. A gal who did the community news items came out and interviewed me for the *Star* — she wanted to know where I stood on teaching machines, sexual intercourse for teen-agers and the new math. I got sent to San Salvador the next week. I never resigned."

"Who did you see today?"

"Beside you, just our columnist friend. He had a note from Campbell's office. It wasn't really an interview; he wanted to tell me why I was wrong on Miró, Ryan, Madera and underestimated the danger of Communism. He didn't bother me with any questions. He planned to leave this evening by chartered plane. I don't think I will see any more reporters. Ambassador Pethwick advised against it. It's been his policy for twenty-four years. Do you find it hot in here?"

It was very hot. Present and perspiring was the newspaperman recommended two days before by Bill O'Donnell. He was visiting Joe Hurd, now the Chargé d'Affaires ad Interim of the Embassy of the United States in Puerto de los Santos, in his apartment in the part of Flores dedicated to Shell, Singer and Bayer drugs and pharmaceuticals. As Counselor of Embassy and Deputy Chief of Mission, Joseph C. Hurd was entitled to what, in formal State Department nomenclature, is called a Representation Dwelling. This is a house in which people of importance can be entertained in a manner befitting the dignity of the United States. But since his wife had left him in disgust some ten years earlier, Joe Hurd had yearned for nothing so ardently as to do no entertaining at all, a desire strengthened by the terrible state of his stomach. On coming to Flores, he had given the house to which he was entitled, an ample structure, deeply influenced by the Esso service station architecture of the late forties — sweeping curves, smooth white walls, flat roof and red cornice — to the Commercial Counselor. The latter was a youngish man with a large family and an excessive optimism on the prospects of increasing dollar earnings in Puerto Santos by building goodwill among potential purchasers. In its place Hurd had taken over a staff apartment downtown, and apart from installing a new air-conditioner had done nothing to make it habitable. It was hideously shabby. The air-conditioner was now off, and the men were sitting in shirt-sleeves in the light of a hurricane lamp borrowed that afternoon from the Embassy storeroom. It made the room even more insufferable, and for the first time Joe Hurd was not entirely sorry that he had been ordered by Mrs. Pethwick to occupy their house and so safeguard her possessions during their absence. He was moving next day. He did not miss the Pethwicks.

"I suppose they are reporting back that Miró is a Red?" Hurd put it as a question.

"There is a difference of opinion. Some are saying that he is a Communist and that the take-over has occurred. A more conservative, or maybe a more liberal, element is giving him the benefit of the doubt. They only say the take-over is imminent."

"Not everyone, I hope."

"There are a few of us — the saving remnant, I believe Matthew Arnold called us — who are avoiding conclusions. It doesn't make for much of a story, and your editor thinks you are missing a bet. Fortunately, my paper doesn't have a strong policy on the Communist menace. The *Time* boys will have to get material for a cover story — Miró with his head bursting through a big red star. Technically it will be quite an achievement and the publisher's page will have a letter praising them. How do you feel about it, Mr. Hurd?"

"You can say Joe. That's in accordance with State Department protocol. Nicknames are used for the brilliantly successful and the deplorable failures. I am, to a singular degree, the last. Bad stomach, no longer able to drink, no social graces, approaching the end of career in, of all places, Puerto Santos. However, many admire the way I accept my fate. It has been the position of this Mission that Martínez, though he had his faults, was a rock of stability. Thus he had our support. Also, all alternatives involved an unacceptable degree of danger. We have no proof that Miró is a Communist, but we have serious misgivings about some of the men around him."

"Do you agree?"

"The question is improper. In our profession, the ambassador must have full authority in his mission. We cannot have a medley of American voices in every capital of the world. Foreigners would be confused. So would Washington. So there must be discipline. However, our diplomatic officers at all levels must show individual initiative and courage and feel completely free to express their own views. I have always endeavored to abide faithfully by both rules. Miró, as I have told O'Donnell unofficially, is a perfectly decent man. Thirty years of dictatorship has left a political and financial vacuum and Miró is just discovering it. Even if his instincts were bad he might be smart enough to know that his one chance for salvation lies with the United States. Neither Moscow nor Peking has what it takes to keep him in office, nor does Fidel Castro. As to the domestic Bolshevists there are only two hundred people in the whole Republic who have heard of Marx, and nearly all of them associate the name with either men's clothing or old movies."

"I don't suppose you want me to quote you on that?"

"No, I would prefer not. Another reason for keeping clear of the press is that my standards of self-censorship are not very severe. But it doesn't matter as much as you think. Whatever you print along these lines, the more knowledgeable people in the Department will say I fed to you. Are you sure you can really stand this heat in here?"

10

A GOVERNMENT CRISIS has this in common with a sex orgy or a drunken bat: The participants greatly enjoy it although they feel they shouldn't. It exhausts them so, one having taken place, another is unlikely to follow immediately. But with the passage of time, one having occurred, there is a heightened possibility of recurrence. For men recover from their exhaustion, and memory improves on past delights.

So it was in Puerto Santos. While Miró worried about the short-run, it was the long-run or, more precisely, the middle-run that was his menace. In the weeks and months following the revolution there was novelty in not having the old dictator any more; instead bright young men were in office. Englishmen are said to have felt the same way in 1837 when suddenly all of the dirty, fat and offensive old kings were gone and they had, instead, a fresh young queen.

The freedom was also enjoyed. This requires explanation. In the most reputable circles in the United States there is a feeling that liberty is most required by those who use it to oppose unnecessary government spending and taxes that penalize private enterprise. For the poor, accordingly, it is not of high importance. Moreover, to Ambassador Pethwick freedom is a somewhat academic concept. He greatly favors the First Amendment. But over many years of professional duty, he has learned to keep a very tight rein on his mind and tongue. He has articulated, often with feeling and sometimes with eloquence, the official position on great issues, always assuming one was available. He has been content in this conformity. He has also been frequently embarrassed by those who speak out of turn. It would be contrary to nature were he to set great store by the right of uninhibited expression. In somewhat more sophisticated form, his views are shared by other old Latin American hands. Of the repressive tendencies of dictators they say: "Yes, quite so. But still the people are happy." Pethwick had often stressed the contentment of the people of Puerto Santos.

Yet, this wisdom notwithstanding, a surprising number of people, other than Anglo-Saxons of good birth and income, enjoy speaking their minds, and though in lesser measure, hearing others do so. They appreciate the associated immunity from arrest. So it was in Puerto Santos. Luis Madera proved to be a man of energy, and once in power he was almost never drunk. The Martínez system of citizen surveillance, based on local informers who were paid by piece rates according to quantity of information provided and funds available, would never have impressed Fritz Kaltenbrunner. In recent years funds had been short and the system had collapsed with the revolution. Madera rounded up several of the more sadistic executives for trial. The police were told to treat people with more consideration, and the better-known exponents of police brutality were culled out and fired. It was a rather stale joke in Flores that as it was ridiculous for their country to have a Ministry of Marine so it was silly for it to have a Ministry of Justice. Madera invited the resignation of the Martínez judges, an invitation coordinate in scope with the whole Puerto Santos judiciary. He reinstated only those of some literacy and with a perceptible interest in distinguishing innocence from guilt. These changes were greeted with enthusiasm that on occasion was extreme. The Dean of the Faculty of Law of the University of Flores, a careful supporter of Martínez for many years and now a strong exponent of personal liberty, took up the most advanced position. "The fundamental spirit of democracy," he told a meeting of the Faculty of Law a few days after the revolution, "proclaims that it is better that a hundred desperate criminals escape than that one innocent man be lodged in jail." He announced that he was inviting Professor Daniel Escobedo to spend a year in Puerto Santos making a study of the criminal code and mentioned their common Spanish antecedents. Somewhere he had got the impression that Escobedo was Dean of the Harvard Law School.

·

There were other accomplishments. The *municipios* were ordered to hold elections to replace the Martínez jobholders, some of whom, forehandedly, had already departed. Other officials were told to treat the public with respect; a few began to reveal a hitherto unrevealed instinct for accomplishment. Miró made a personal appeal to the notably languorous public employees and sent a more rigorous communication to their department heads. Once again gangs of men were to be seen out mending streets and roads. The malarial swamps back of Santos were sprayed for mosquitoes for the first time in several years, and despite the misgivings of the new Minister of Natural Resources, a devotee of the late Miss Rachel Carson, as to the dangers of DDT. The drainage ditches through the slums there and in Flores were opened up. The water mains were repaired, and water ran once more from the community spigots. A ceiling was set on the rent that could be charged for the tin-roofed shacks, and, to emphasize the point, a few weeks later four landlords in Flores and two in Santos were hauled before the new judges and awarded a stiff fine for violation. They were deeply indignant, less at the fine than that their owner-ship of this depressing property should have been made known. Who could say how people might react? The tenants and laborers out in the country were told that they would get land. The electricity was turned on, and, al-though the newspapermen had by this time vacated the big hotel on the hill, the elevators now ran and so did the water faucets, and, with prudence, the toilets could be flushed.

There was, astonishingly enough, a modest revival of business in Flores. For years business firms, foreign and domestic alike, had conducted all activities with one eye to the depredations of the Martínez regime. To leave money in the country for as much as overnight seemed to some unsafe. Now there was a slight feeling of security. And while Puerto Santos did not look to importer or trader, foreign or domestic, like an especially brilliant economic prospect, it did seem a good idea to cover bets. If one didn't, there was always the danger that someone else would get a stranglehold. Accordingly, to beat the Japanese, the Germans and Dutch came in. This aroused the interest of the French and Italians. Eventually, a few British and American firms heard that something was stirring. It was no great revival, but things were better than for several years.

•

Surprisingly enough, one of the initial successes was Roberto Ryan. If there is anything that the people of Puerto Santos want, more than anything else, it is schools. This is not because of intellectual curiosity or an original commitment to the enlightenment. It is simply because, like people almost everywhere else, they have observed that men who can read and write can usually get jobs and those who have gone longest to school get the best jobs, including those that can be performed sitting down. Nearly every man in Puerto Santos has at some time or another looked for a job and has been asked about his education. So, there is no part of the Republic where people are so backward that they do not understand its advantages.

Roberto Ryan scrounged a few thousand dollars for

books and brought them from Mexico City. He then set about organizing those who could read and write as committees of public instruction. The idea was simple; the committee selected one of its numbers as a principal. Under his or her leadership they rounded up the children of the village or police precinct and parceled out the job of providing instruction.

They did it free, but Ryan devised a system of deferred reward. He promised those who did well that they would get certificates and eventually jobs as regular teachers. The few fully literate officials in the Ministry of Education were sent around to supervise. The somewhat less literate were also sent out to teach. In the Martínez days there had been a small Peace Corps contingent in Puerto Santos. The old man had always been careful, on minor points, to persuade Washington of his incipient idealism. Now it came into its own, and reinforcements were even diverted from Chile, Costa Rica and Venezuela. They were distributed around as a kind of stiffening to the system and plunged into their tasks with great enthusiasm and some competence.

Roberto Ryan's educational system may well have been the worst in the free or otherwise world. Many believed that he was exploiting the passion for schooling for his own political advancement, although in the past such advancement had never been thought dependent on effort of any kind. In time, it seemed certain the volunteer pedagogues would get tired; in the absence of pay they would fade away. In the rainy season it would not be possible to hold classes under a palm tree. Still, for the

time being, it gave the country the best system of public
education it had ever had. Indeed it was its first.

These accomplishments were neither inconsiderable
nor unrecognized. But they had two features in common.
All could be done with no or very little money. All were
limited by the general shortage of money. It followed
that things that depended on money could not be done at
all.

·

The matter of money came up, as frequently before, at a
meeting between the Provisional President and his Finance Minister one morning something under six months
after the revolution. Sr. Medina was on the point of de-
parting for Washington. He had not done badly in his
brief period in office. Enough funds had been scraped
up to pay the army and most of the public officials, although one payroll had been passed in early November.
A certain attrition among the public servants had helped,
and the Minister had found it helpful, for dispensing with
purely decorative officials, to explain that no money for
pay was available or in sight. Now tax revenues promised
to cover, though just barely, the functionally or politically
essential payroll. That meant that nothing was left over for
other things—for housing, hospitals, schools or roads. It
meant that the army was on tight rations. There was no
money for new equipment and not much for gasoline
for the existing trucks, jeeps, staff cars and tanks. There
was none for spare parts and new uniforms; there was
none to replace the wear and tear in barracks and mess;

worst of all, there was none to freshen the myriad of financial rivulets from which the defenders of Puerto Santos were accustomed to improve their modest salaries. In other words, graft was badly off.

There had been pleas to Washington to resume aid, notably the much-relished cash support to the Puerto Santos budget and the military assistance. The Special Representative dispatched to Washington after the revolution had, by his own account, tried valiantly. Washington had not been forthcoming. Now Sr. Medina was on his way.

"You must impress on them the grave urgency of our need. I rely on you fully." It was the President, and he spoke with a passion that is no more reliably occasioned by deprivation in love than by a shortage of liquid assets.

"They already know how much we need help. I had a talk with the good Hurd the other day, and he hinted that that was just the trouble."

"How do you mean?" asked the President.

"The Americans have an old and vulgar folk-saying. It is about a man having his ass in a meat grinder."

"Go on. I'm never sure that you clarify things with your parables."

"When a man is known to be in this awkward as well as obscene situation, others establish, as it were, a certain physical and moral authority over his behavior."

"You mean Washington wants to keep me in its power?"

"They would not put it so crudely," said the Minister. "In my experience, not many of our friends in the United States enjoy the crude exercise of power and even fewer like to admit to its employment. They wish to be assured, only, that you are deeply committed to the cause of democracy and the free world. You have seen what the American papers say about our regime."

"Everybody knows that I am not a Communist. What in the name of God do I have to do to reassure them? I am trying only to keep a few of my promises."

"Some American officials, we must face it, are not easy to reassure. If you are not a Communist, they suspect you of being a fellow traveler. If you are not a fellow traveler, they suspect you of being a stooge. If you are too smart to be a stooge, they suspect you of being a stalking horse. If assured on all these counts, they will still conclude that you are an opening to the left."

"Well, you must reassure them," said the President with some emphasis. "Now, how about this idea of getting some help from the World Bank, the IDA, the United Nations Special Fund or your International Monetary Fund?"

"The United Nations agencies in my experience are reluctant to act in opposition to the United States. It provides them with upward of a third of all their money."

"You have the sugar quota in mind and allowing our cattle into the Puerto Rico market? I am being pressed very hard about sugar and cattle prices."

"I have these very much in mind. Success here will also depend on our ability to reassure the State Department. It has the last word. The same is true of any steps we can take on the Martínez properties. I promise you that I will do my best. It is not easy for one elderly man to move the entire city of Washington."

"My good friend, from the bottom of my heart I wish you luck."

"It is not entirely surprising that you should, Mr. President. If you will allow me the liberties of what both the Japanese and the Americans call an elder statesman, I would like to point out that the bottom of your heart is not, anatomically speaking, so far removed from the jaws of that meat grinder."

.

Toward eleven o'clock that same evening the Provisional President had a second meeting about American assistance. It was with General Pérez. The General came immediately to the point.

"I hear old Medina is going to Washington tomorrow."

"That is correct. In point of fact, he left this afternoon."

"You must tell him to get our military aid back."

"Queen Elizabeth of England once reminded one of her ministers that 'must' is not a word that you use to princes. Likewise it is not a word a country of our size uses to Washington. Do sit down, General."

The General eased the outer edge of his broad bottom onto the front few inches of a chair. He couldn't use more or his feet would stick out to the front. He was careful of his dignity.

"I wasn't speaking to Washington. I was speaking to you."

"Are you by some chance fearing an attack by Colombia, Panama, Guatemala? Honduras? Maybe Nicaragua?"

"The Americans give our neighbors arms. We must get them too. It is their system of mutual insecurity. Besides, soldiers that do not get new weapons have poor morale."

"And their officers do not make money on parts and repairs and the sale of the old ones?"

"Mr. President, this is not a joking matter. I am very, very serious. And so are my comrades-in-arms. The army needs gasoline, spare parts, supplies of all kinds. And I must mention another thing."

"Please do. I would gather you have enough food."

If the General heard the observation, he ignored it. "Something is happening among the younger officers. I do not know what it is, but it could be very bad for you and everyone."

"Are they not getting their cut?"

"I repeat this is not a matter for joking, Mr. President. I must warn you. And it is not a financial problem. It is talk I do not understand. They say that not enough progress is being made. They believe that your government lacks courage to tackle the fundamental problems of the Republic."

"I would gladly trade a little courage for some money. What do they want me to do? Take over the Martínez properties? Declare war on the United States? Give Aragón your job?"

"I do not know what they want. There are many rumors. I hear even I am criticized. It may be that I am considered too friendly to you. My own people are uneasy. They think we should have a government that can get help from the United States. They hear the Americans think we are going Communist. Mr. President, I warn you as a friend; we are loyal officers, but we cannot tolerate subversive agitation. We must have a government that pleases the Americans and stops this agitation in the army."

It was quite a speech, one of the longest the Minister of National Defense had ever made. He was audibly out of breath when he finished. The Provisional President gazed at the General for several long moments. It was well to give him the impression that he was being taken seriously. Then speaking with rather deliberate care, he replied:

"There are many kinds of friendship, my dear General, including, it is said, those that make even enemies unnecessary. I value your friendship for all that it is worth. Naturally, I am much impressed by what you have told me. We are making the strongest possible effort in Washington. That includes your guns and gasoline. Now perhaps you will allow me a word of friendly advice. I am not a Communist, and I am not encouraging Communism among your young officers. And the people in Washington in these last years have often spoken out in favor of civilian governments in this part of the world. I hope, still speaking as a friend, you will keep this in mind."

The two men shook hands. Miró observed that there was a little extra pressure in the General's grip. It was obvious that his closing words on friendship had touched his visitor. The General departed. The President wondered why Puerto Santos generals always looked a little ridiculous. Too many ribbons? Too much braid? Did they sleep in their uniforms? Were they all untidy eaters? Certainly they should be taller, cleaner-shaven and much thinner. Was it simply because for them soldiering was an afterthought? He had not noticed these things when he was a cadet. He rang for his secretary.

"We need to get a message off to Medina," he said when the young man came in. "The army seems to be forming up on both the left and the right. Could you guess who might be in the middle?"

11

THE CHANCERY OF THE AMERICAN EMBASSY occupies three floors in the Shell Building. Of all the square buildings of stained concrete and dirty glass in downtown Flores, this is perhaps the most depressing. Except for the Great Seal of the United States on the door, the fact that the desks are of the standard olive green favored for the official proletariat for the last forty years by the Commissioner of the Federal Supply Service of the General Services Administration and before that by the Procurement Division of the Treasury, and that chairs and sofas are of excellent brown leather and uniform design, little distinguishes these offices from the local headquarters of the oil company below. The Ambassador's residence, however, is on the side of the hill on a small street just off the road leading to the big hotel. It is altogether pleasant.

The house was built during the nineteen-twenties before the days of air-conditioning by a Flores merchant of Jewish extraction and excellent taste. The public rooms are large with high ceilings and are shaded by wide verandas. These, in turn, are protected from the sun by strips of lattice stretching from roof to floor and by the rich tropical foliage in the garden. Between the palms one has an excellent view of the old city and the white marble palace. Where the Pethwicks had hoped, one day, to have a swimming pool, there is a croquet course. In a number of capitals the Congress has been persuaded to appropriate money for swimming pools for ambassadors on the theory that the water so stored is an added safeguard in the event of fire. Protection is thus simultaneously provided against loss and the charge that money is being spent on a Hollywood standard of living. In Flores, however, over much of the year, mildew is much more of a hazard than fire, and, as the experience of the big hotel so sadly attests, the municipal water supply is not sufficiently reliable to offset evaporation from a pool. Also the priority of Puerto Santos is inherently low.

The furniture of the house, until comparatively recent times, was of rush, reed and rattan and matched in coolness the spacious rooms. There was always an abundance of tropical flowers and plants in the rooms and on the verandas, and they added the light and color that was otherwise lacking. However, it has been Mrs. Pethwick's pride, as a veteran of twenty-five years in the Foreign Service, that she "always takes with her the things she loves." The State Department pays for such transport, so no financial sacrifice is involved. The objects of her affection, unfortunately, include quite a few rather heavy overstuffed pieces in walnut and mahogany and some especially massive chairs, dining table, cabinets, break-fronts, secretaries and other woodenware which, according to family legend, her ancestors toted from Virginia across Kentucky when they first established themselves in Illinois. They must have been a heavy burden for her ancestors as they are on this pleasant house. Mrs. Pethwick allows everyone to assume that either her forebears or Pethwick's also brought with them the half-dozen heavily varnished, stiff-collared, angry and possibly psychotic ancestors who look down with manifest disapproval from the walls. However, when the Pethwicks were in Korea, a knowledgeable young Englishman of dubious inclinations from the British mission identified one of them as a portrait, possibly posthumous, of Lord Peel. And when they were being unpacked in Flores an aide to the Ambassador found on the back of another a small and long-neglected tag bearing the name of a Chicago secondhand dealer. But, ancestors or otherwise, Mrs. Pethwick loves the paintings, too.

On the evening of the day of the Finance Minister's departure, three men had just taken the only places set at one end of the massive mahogany table below the putative ancestor from South State Street. Two were in shirt-sleeves with loosened neckties. The third, wearing a bush shirt that might have been of his own design, was Joe Hurd who was breaking ever so slightly his rule against entertaining. The youngest of the three they addressed as Captain. A Spanish-American named González, he had been appointed to West Point by the late Senator Chávez of New Mexico and made Assistant Army Attaché in Flores because he spoke Spanish. It was not known that he would come to consider men like Martínez an insult to all people of Latin origin. His connections among the younger officers of the Puerto Santos army were excellent. The other man, a few years younger than Hurd, was a guest over from the big hotel. His eyes ranged around the room, returned briefly the disapproving stare of each of the ancestors, then he said to Hurd:

"Secure?"

The answer from Hurd similarly reflected the succinct professionalism of the times. "Swept last week." With a trace of apology in his voice he added, "There never has been any bugging here, I'm sorry to say. I know it's an invasion of privacy, but it does indicate a certain position in the world." For a moment all reflected on their inferiority, and then Joe Hurd went on, his voice appreciably brighter, "Martínez did have a boy once who listened in on our calls during working hours. Once he heard the Secretary tell the Ambassador that he was having trouble over aid with Wayne Morse. Martínez called personally to check the Senator's name and get his price. Ambassador Pethwick was rather troubled. It was the first time he ever had to turn down a request from Martínez."

The stranger's eyes were still on a portrait. "We should give one of those to each of our former employees. She would remind them to keep their mouth shut. It's my feeling, my boy, that you statesmen had better get around fairly soon to giving your blessing to Miró along with some money. Otherwise he is going to come unglued."

"Reveal your secrets." It was Hurd.

"Let me first explain the laws of intelligence according to Dulles, McCone, Bond and the other immortals of our craft. First, you can learn very little about the future of a government that doesn't know its own intentions. Second, in Latin America there are no secrets, just a general shortage of information. But I hear the old generals are getting restive — no new toys, no graft; they barely get their pay and missed that a few weeks back. And there seems now to be a Young Turks movement. Not a secret in the whole sack. I did hear that Pérez intends to lay down the law to Miró. What have you heard about the young officers, Captain?"

"There is certainly a faction that feels . . . well, let down." The Captain paused for a moment and then went on a bit more assertively, "No one will believe that there are idealists in a Latin American army, I know."

"Youth," said Joe Hurd. "You simply can't tell where it will break out these days. What do they want?"

"Not General Pérez," said the Captain. "If they are for Castro, they naturally don't tell me. What some want is more action out of Miró. I couldn't agree more on the need to get behind him. What is holding us up?"

"Fear of Communism, Captain," said Hurd. "Do you know about that? I have recommended restoration of full relations and some real money. A few people in Washington are for it. Bill O'Donnell is for it. So are the boys in the White House, I hear. So are OAS people. But nothing doing."

"Why?"

"That is where you younger men are weak. You do not

understand about blind spots the way we old Communist fighters do. Multiple interconnected blind spots really. Miró is believed by Washington to have a blind spot where Communism is concerned. So when I argue that Miró is okay, it means that I have a blind spot where Miró is concerned. O'Donnell argues that I am right. It follows that he has a blind spot where I am concerned. Besides he is a Catholic, and Catholics are now thought to have a special blind spot where Communism is concerned — that includes the Pope. The boys at the White House are sympathetic. That is because they have a general blind spot resulting from inexperience. In other words, all who disagree with the official line are disqualified by blind spots. They are a great handicap."

Joe Hurd finally came to a halt, and Captain González looked confused. Diffidently, he ventured, "I still think they should trust the people who know. What have they got to lose?"

"That," said Joe Hurd with emphasis, "is precisely the problem. They have a great deal to lose. Not me. I have been too long in grade and will soon be selected out. A real honor. But not O'Donnell. When he is asked if he can guarantee that Miró will never be taken over by the Communists, he probably hesitates a trifle. And his hesitation is noticed. He has heard what happened to the guys who underestimated Mao and Castro. Indecent assault on others of the same sex and underestimating Communists are the two things our Service neither forgives nor forgets. Besides the men who are thought to know are not with us but against us, and it is the reputation for knowing that really counts. Ambassador Pethwick is against us, and he is fresh from the scene. Worth Campbell is against us, and his experience with Communism is as old as the Czar's and more successful. The Secretary is against us, and he has detected the hand of Communists in every attack on the United States since the Alamo. That's the picture, Captain."

"You know," said the stranger, "up until the time I left Washington, Miró did not have a completely bad press."

"Yeah. But in the early days it was made pretty clear that putting Madera in charge of the police and Ryan in education were part of a pattern. And Aragón got a large billing. At that point Puerto Santos ceased to be news, and people stopped reading about it. The basic view was set. Miró remains a Communist stooge. Anyhow suppose he did sell himself to the *New York Times,* Washington *Post* and Baltimore *Sun.* That only shows the inexperience of these reporters and what they will do to write a different story. All have a blind spot. They also believe that I am feeding ideas to some of them. My one claim to influence."

"I hear the Finance Minister is leaving tomorrow for one more effort. They won't think he is a Communist?"

"Medina left tonight actually. No, not a Communist. Not a fellow traveler. Not inexperienced. I think he will be dismissed as an old man past his best. Age has given him a blind spot."

"Well," said the stranger, "my agency never makes policy. But I could buck up a tactfully worded appreciation saying that Miró is a good man trying to do a job and that we can expect worse to happen if we don't get the rag out. A straight intelligence estimate, that's all."

"Everyone will appreciate your reticence," said Hurd. "Many will think it unprecedented. I wish you would. I will get off another of my pro-Communist missives to my fellow diplomats. I don't guess, Captain, that we can get the army in on this plot. How is life up at the hotel?"

"Our regulations require inconspicuous residence," replied the stranger. "I think I am complying. No one can possibly believe the place is habitable."

·

In addition to the man who had come down from the big hotel to dine with Joe Hurd, there had been another equally inconspicuous visitor in Puerto Santos during the preceding week. He had returned — or rather continued on — to Washington two or three days before the Finance Minister. A serious and diligent man, he had promptly completed, revised and submitted his report. The man was Dr. Richard Williams Kent, Special Consultant on Primary and Secondary Educational Methods and Programs for the Agency for International Development. He had one thing in common with General Pérez. Puerto Santos generals are generally thought of as being untidy, short and fat. American educators are characteristically lean, sallow and slightly shrunken about the cheekbones. Both General Pérez and Dr. R. W. Kent were caricatures of their stereotype.

The AID missions of the United States, according to ideal, are staffed by young and dedicated men and

women who are impelled by conscience and the love of
adventure to spend their life in the service of mankind
in distant lands. This is sometimes so. But most of the
young and dedicated have children in school, careers in
which they take a thoughtful interest, laboratories they
cannot desert, universities which will not grant them an
indefinite leave of absence, rich but ailing relatives who
require unsubtle affection, or it has happened that conscience and love of adventure are distributed unequally
across the marriage ties. That is to say, the man's wife
greatly prefers East Lansing or Ames. In consequence,
many of the scientists and technicians who serve abroad
have reached retirement age in their university, college of
agriculture, experiment station, agricultural extension service, engineering firm or industrial laboratory. Their
children are on their own. Their parents are dead. Retired, they are a bit *passé*, and they are also very short
of income. So they readily agree to spend a few years
serving in some new and aspiring land. Some are very distinguished. Some are not. Some cannot be classified, for
while they were very distinguished at home, they are
the reverse beyond our borders. Dr. R. W. Kent was one
who did not lend himself to classification.

A Ph.D. from Teachers College of Columbia University,
he had been successively Professor of Education, Director of Educational Research and Associate Dean for Educational Projects and Research at the University of Missouri from which he had himself been graduated with
modest distinction in the class of 1921. He measured the
world by the closeness with which it conformed to proved

practices in the better school districts in the State of Missouri. For some months, he had been serving with a team studying the primary educational system of Ecuador. On his way home, he had asked Washington for permission to stop over to see the new educational experiments in Puerto Santos. Although the AID mission there had been reduced to a standby basis, Washington could see no harm. A visit by Dr. Kent could not, by any stretch of imagination, be construed by Miró as implying Washington approval. There was some interest in what he might learn about Ryan's endeavors.

The trip had been in many ways a disaster. A more experienced man would have notified the Flores Embassy from Quito of his expected time of arrival. Dr. Kent relied on Washington. In consequence, he arrived unannounced at the Flores airport and, after an expensive taxi trip into town, at the Embassy. He asked to see the Ambassador, not knowing or at least not recalling that Pethwick had been withdrawn, and eventually wound up in Joe Hurd's office. The Chargé was sipping milk and in poor humor. Since he was prevented for professional reasons from venting it on his own staff or the people of Puerto Santos, he brought it willingly to bear on, as he saw it, an unnecessary bureaucrat from an inferior agency. He asked the desolate and, for the moment, quite inarticulate Dr. Kent why in hell his agency did not have the courtesy to tell him they were sending visitors; why it went around making useless academic studies; why instead of inspecting these improvised and pathetic schools, it didn't give the poor bastards some money.

Dr. Kent was unable to respond on any of these points, and though Hurd eventually relented to the extent of providing a car to take his visitor up to the hotel, the latter's first impression of Puerto Santos was very poor. Fortunately Joe Hurd's age and his generally disreputable appearance kept Dr. Kent from associating him with the nasty young men — he always assumed from Princeton or Yale — who had made his life miserable in Fort Lamy, Monrovia, and one or two other desolate capitals to which he had gone in line of educational duty. At the hotel his room at this time of year was comfortably cool; but when he went into the bathroom two elephantine cockroaches went to ground in the chasm back of the basin, and the smell was far from reassuring. In truth, the hotel had not yet recovered from the period of heavy patronage months earlier when it had been without water.

The next day had been much worse. The car which the hotel ordered for him did not come until noon. The driver did not know the new schools existed, much less where they were to be found, and had only an indifferent knowledge of English. Courteously, he had taken Dr. Kent to a whorehouse on Paseo Roosevelt. Dr. Kent ascertained that it was not, as might conceivably have been imagined, a seminary for young ladies. The driver had then taken him to Casas San Luis e San Miguel after which Dr. Kent, with great reluctance, was reduced to seeking the help of the Embassy. Fortunately Joe Hurd was feeling better.

When he got to the schools, he had difficulty appraising their operations. At the first, all activity came to a halt on his arrival, and at the second, despite the entreaties of the teacher, the children hastily decamped. Dr. Kent also spoke no Spanish.

The meeting with the Education Minister which Joe Hurd obligingly set up for the following day was even less satisfactory. The Ryans had lost their command of English, if so it could ever have been described, several generations back. But this the Minister did not concede, and he sought to make up in speed and vehemence for what he lacked in vocabulary, pronunciation and syntax. He was very hard to follow. But even this imperfect communication was sufficient to establish that he had never heard of two-track systems, achievement scores, verbal aptitude tests, SAT's, motivation-enhancing mechanisms, or even dropout ratios. Instead he harped tediously on his need for money and the meanness of the Americans in cutting off aid. Dr. Kent tried to explain with no success that these matters were outside his area of responsibility.

Very possibly Dr. Kent's frustrations influenced his report. This was unfortunate, for it could have been the first report of the Agency for International Development on the subject of education to have had any considerable readership beyond those who drafted it, those who checked it for factual content, those who processed it for consistency of program content, those who reviewed it for applicability of policy recommendation, and the girl who did the typing. It read, in very limited part, as follows:

> . . . of course recognize that this country does not have the financial resources and money to build to

the better norms of the modern American school district. Nevertheless, almost no attention seems to have been given to the systematic upgrading of educational plant and equipment. Teaching on brief inspection seemed to be confined to elementary reading and letter-forming with very low aspirational horizons as regards further development. It is clearly nonprofessional and lacking in conceptual depth. . . .

(15) In course of a long conversation with the Minister I confirmed the impression that he is lacking in conceptual depth. He is almost totally ignorant of modern educational methodology and systems and also indifferent to these concepts. He is narrowly oriented to money, finances and budgetary issues. Much of the meeting was characterized by expressions of extreme hostility to the United States. His statements in the judgment of this analyst reflect a fairly fundamental conditioning in anti-American attitudes. . . .

(17) It is concluded that despite its extensive publicity the Puerto Santos educational program is probably over-publicized. It cannot be considered a serious educational program as a modern educator would evaluate it. It is probably to be categorized as a personal political propaganda program of the present Minister of Education. . . .

12

IN THE WEEKS THAT FOLLOWED the revolution, the system of social statics that so unexpectedly protected Miró brought no comfort to Worth Campbell. He outlined his fears one morning to Symes Jones. As with all men who ask questions and listen carefully to the answers, people passed many pleasant hours explaining things to Symes Jones. That he was educated in proportion to the hours so spent is uncertain.

The first days of a crisis are not, Campbell had pointed out, the really dangerous ones from the standpoint of the free world interest. Then the experienced newsmen are attentive or on the spot. Public attention is fixed on the danger point. All this insures that it will be viewed with anxiety and even alarm. There may be some danger of excessive excitement, of overreaction.

Then the newsmen leave, and the next crisis ensues. Public attention shifts. Now the real threat arises.

"You remember when Vice-President Nixon got into trouble in Caracas. All his friends and admirers were worried; they thought he was going to get caught in a Communist take-over. But there wasn't much danger. Everyone was watching and greatly worried, and the President himself alerted the Marines. In Panama a few years ago, when there were riots over our schoolchildren flying the American flag, the Secretary himself warned it was the Communists who were stirring things up. When they tried to bring back Bosch in the Dominican Republic, and he looked pretty questionable, we were willing to send in troops. In a crisis we are alert even when, as it developed in those cases, the Communists aren't really involved. But later on any of these places could be in real danger, and no one would be watching." Symes Jones had nodded intelligently and asked the Assistant Secretary when he judged the time of real danger would come in Puerto Santos.

This was not yet clear, but it was certain that things were proceeding according to Worth Campbell's expectations. The reporters who had flocked there as a fire brigade were, naturally, men who needed to justify the substitution of movement for thought. It was on this that their livelihood depended. Accordingly, they had not minimized the extent and depth of the danger. Nor had the television people when the crew had been fleshed out to strength. The names of Madera and Ryan, and also of Aragón (variously called "one Carlos," "an individual named" and by a wire-service man after hastily consulting the wrong Spanish reference, "Ancien Estado") had come prominently into the news. If Campbell had a problem at this stage, it was to keep highly valuable concern about what was occurring from leading to overly severe action.

But the take-over, so abundantly predicted, had not occurred. The few reporters who had remained on in Flores had talked with Miró and also with Madera and Ryan. They had formed a generally favorable impression of what Miró and Madera were trying to do — they had even had a good word for Roberto Ryan. Then journeyman pundits with indistinct assignments from *The New Republic, Commentary, The Progressive* and *The New Leader* had passed through. Their reports had been uniformly favorable to Miró and either egregiously optimistic or hopelessly pessimistic about his prospects. Joe Hurd had contributed, perhaps more than he realized, to the reassuring view of Miró and his men. He saw few of these reporters. But all heard that he was a defender of Miró. If the resident Department of State official defends a man, it is hard for anyone to feel that he is a Communist or even an opening to the left.

So the tendency to relax was now Worth Campbell's problem. The danger remained, people were much less alert, and one knew that the best of observers could be had by the Communists. Once a highly experienced reporter from the Baltimore *Sun,* a man who knew the realities of life, had dropped into Campbell's office in Paris; he was on his way home from Italy where he had talked with Togliatti. He had been charmed by Togliatti's candor and had thought the Communist leader sincere when he said that he often differed with Moscow and doubted that Italy would soon go Communist. This Campbell never forgot.

Whatever else was true of Puerto Santos, Madera and Ryan were still in their jobs.

A few days after the ejection of Martínez, Worth Campbell had testified before a closed session of the full Senate Foreign Relations Committee. He had gone over the general lines of his testimony at a meeting in the Secretary's office, and the White House had seen the prepared statement. He had summarized policy on Miró — even the Assistant Secretary did not feel that the words conveyed any great sense of novelty — as one of "watchful waiting." Alarm in these days was still acute although not as great as one would have expected.

Over the years Campbell, like many others, had come to think of the Congress of the United States as a bastion of committed anti-Communism. Here one's problem was really to keep legislators from carrying alarm to reckless or unproductive lengths. You didn't worry about people who thought you too hard-nosed and tough. This criticism was so rare and so cautious and so muted on Capitol Hill that it could be ignored. You worried about the man who stood for the right policy but carried it to extremes — who wanted to cut off all trade with the bastards, sever diplomatic relations, send in the Air Force, drop the Bomb and who thought you a security case, at a minimum softheaded, if you demurred.

But less now than formerly. At the Senate hearing several of the younger members had asked, though politely, if Miró shouldn't be given a chance, and one of the senior

members, an irascible liberal with a long interest in Latin American affairs, had strongly attacked Pethwick for
his undeviating support of Martínez. The Assistant Secretary, when he thought of the matter at all, considered
himself a Democrat, his votes for Ike and Nixon notwithstanding. But few people were so unpractical in their approach to foreign policy, so lacking in a grasp of hard
realities, as the liberal Democrats. In spite of himself he
had had a feeling of relief that day when the questioning
shifted south and to the Republicans. When one of the
latter said, "Doctor, about this 'watchful waiting.' It
doesn't mean that you will just sit on your asses down
there — strike that — I mean duffs — until the Communists take over, does it?" The Assistant Secretary had allowed himself a responding smile and assured the Senator
it did not. He had been equally grateful for the next question.

"Doctor, can you tell me from your experience if it is a
well-organized tactic of the Communist conspiracy to begin by getting control of the educational system and the
police?" Worth Campbell had replied that it was dangerous to generalize, but that this had certainly been a
pattern. There was nothing rigid about Communist tactics. On the next question, however, he had applied the
brakes.

"Doctor, I appreciate your having to be careful in this
matter. Now, is it not a fact that in this country this new
man Miró has put two well-known and proclaimed Communists in charge of education and the police?" The
questioner had permitted himself a glance at his col-

leagues. There had been the slight hush that always marks the really significant question.

"I think it would be premature, Senator, to say that they are proclaimed Communists," Campbell had replied. Then, measuring his words, he had continued. "I can tell you that we are keeping the situation under very close scrutiny. Very close. I certainly can say we are concerned." Even O'Donnell, who was along, was agreeably surprised at his cautious tone. Had the Committee called O'Donnell to the witness chair, they would have received a different and not unuseful view of developments in Puerto Santos. That the Committee did not contemplate nor did O'Donnell expect it. God is known to assign intelligence somewhat at random. But in the United States government godless and god-fearing agree that it must be exploited strictly in accordance with official rank.

.

In the weeks following the Senate hearing, Puerto Santos passed from the news, and, according to Worth Campbell's calculation, the extent of the danger thus further increased. As opportunity presented itself, he warned of the continuing danger. One excellent chance presented itself when Pethwick was invited to attend an off-the-record session of the Council on Foreign Relations in New York. The policy was to keep Pethwick under wraps. His past commitment to Martínez invited questions. However well answered, which in the case of Pethwick could not be guaranteed, the questions reminded people of things that could usefully be forgotten. Campbell had the invitation shifted to himself. He also enjoyed attending meetings of the Council.

Like all meetings this was in the Council's headquarters in the Harold Pratt house on Park Avenue. The Pratts were nearly the last of the independent oil men to surrender to the monopoly of Standard Oil and the first Rockefeller. The terms were magnificent and so accordingly is the house that Harold Pratt built in 1919. So especially is the library, with its handsome portraits of past leaders of American foreign policy, deep rugs, gleaming mahogany and two towering floors of bookshelves with a gallery surrounding the second. It was here, rather than in a larger room, that this meeting was held. Puerto Santos enlists the interest only of the more devoted members.

The devoted membership of the Council includes a few Columbia University professors and a number of former Under Secretaries and Assistant Secretaries of the Departments of State and Defense for whom it continues a nostalgic association with an experience that all found more exciting although financially less remunerative than the practice of law to which they have since reluctantly returned. It also includes a larger number of lawyers and business executives with no Washington experience who are genuinely interested in foreign affairs, or who feel guilty about their primary preoccupation with making money, or who hope to inform themselves of developments yet unknown to the public, out of which they can make money or who hope to secure new clients or make useful friends. Those who seek information are of some slight concern to the elder statesmen of the Council for there is a question whether public officials should provide them, in confidence, with intelligence that other and equally necessitous lawyers or executives are not allowed to hear. Nor do they like to rely on the obvious justification which is that little information of any novelty is ever imparted. This, sadly, is the case. Speeches or articles on foreign policy almost never depend for their interest on their contents. They almost always depend on the importance of the author. Naturally not much is missed by those who are not allowed to hear an authoritative exposition of the already known.

In his mature years Worth Campbell had found the Council a great aid to morale. At the university, at the White House, now in the Senate and in the persons of Bill O'Donnell, Joe Hurd and other younger Foreign Service officers he had found that unclarity of view about Communism and the Cold War which increasingly had blighted his later life. At the Council, he found reassurance. It was still dominated, almost as an alumni association by the men who served with him in Berlin and Paris or under Dulles. They understood and accepted, as did Worth Campbell, the clear lessons of their own experience. They mistrusted those who were not similarly qualified. Perhaps some younger men had doubts. They did not voice them for, naturally, they wanted to establish the kind of confidence among their elders that produces friends or even clients.

In this sympathetic environment Worth Campbell had warned frankly about Madera and Ryan and the ability of Miró to control them. He reminded his audience of the pattern of past Communist tactics and added his purely personal opinion that the two cabinet officers were biding their time. This meant that Puerto Santos was still a trouble spot. He spoke of the unwisdom of taking at face value some of the newspaper accounts now coming out of Puerto Santos. Most of those present, he felt, would suppose that he had the *New York Times* in mind, and he could not be sorry. He dropped back again to remind the younger men present how Communism had come to Czechoslovakia under Jan Masaryk. There, too, people had relaxed and had learned, too late, what control of key ministries by the Communists could mean.

The first question, when the time came for discussion, was, "Do you see, sir, the likelihood of military action in this area?"

On this, Worth Campbell was more cautious. To be explicit in such a prediction was to risk having it remembered — and, at second or third hand, relayed to the newspapers. No meeting attended by seventy-five men is ever completely secure. He replied that there had been contingency planning; that the Air Force was continuing to develop its techniques for combining bombing with a strong appeal to the sympathies of the civilian population. Nothing was more important than effective counter-insurging action of this kind. But as everyone realized, military intervention in this part of the world was not to be entered upon too lightly.

On restoring full diplomatic relations and resuming economic assistance, he had been a good deal more specific. All intelligence indicated, he said, that Miró was beginning to feel the pinch. His representative in Washington was pressing very hard for resumption of aid. "We think," he said in summary, "that the present policy is hurting." It was the first time he had quite got around to saying that to hurt was his intention.

The questions continued. Outside on Park Avenue the late afternoon traffic ground to a halt, and the horns spoke their impatience. People on the sidewalks waved hopelessly at full taxis. Taxi drivers ignored them. A sharp breeze stirred the heavy air and, on occasion, the garbage along the edge of the street. The city was passing through its twice-daily agony of movement. But within, Worth Campbell had only a sense of warmth, good order, dignity and careful thought. "Do you foresee the possibility of President Martínez's return? What, sir, is the longer-run picture for foreign investment in Puerto Santos? Will Miró seize the Martínez properties? What is the present role of Castro infiltration? Could you give us, Mr. Secretary, some details on this man Aragón? What, would you say, is the prospect for development under private enterprise?" The questions were grave and deferential and bespoke the reasonable and informed view. Worth Campbell warmed to his surroundings; his answers, prudent, undidactic, circumstantial and always addressed as to equals suggested authority and inspired confidence. Campbell himself could not help feeling that this was the way foreign policy should be discussed and conducted. It is not something to be resolved in a harsh, vulgar clash of opinion. It is something to be taken up by experts who share a common, clearheaded view of the world, and it does not hurt if they are gentlemen.

.

Afterward, men making their way up Park Avenue, over to the East Side, or riding out to New Rochelle or Port Washington, made a mental note to keep a closer eye on Puerto Santos. The more susceptible felt an agreeable shiver of alarm over the impending disasters to which they were privy. One morning they would wake up to read that Madera's police had moved in on a populace conditioned by Ryan's propaganda. Castro and the Russians would have recognized the new regime. The name of Aragón would be on all lips. Or they would read of the steps by which the United States had forestalled this disaster. In either case, it would come as no surprise. Those with impressionable or patient wives, or more ambiguous dinner companions, framed in their minds the report they would render on the revelations of Worth Campbell.

Worth Campbell had dinner with a friend from Paris days, now opulent, admiring and serene as a member of a big downtown law firm. On the all-but-deserted shuttle back to Washington he picked a *Newsweek* out of the magazine rack and discarded it. It was two weeks old, and someone had torn out a several-page feature on the present legal position of pornography. He glanced briefly at a copy of *Nation's Business* for late the previous summer. It was also a trifle grimy and warned that excessive government spending was leading inevitably to higher taxes and, ultimately, to the brink of national bankruptcy. He looked in his dispatch case, but he had a firm rule against carrying classified documents. Once, in his European days, he had unaccountably left an *Official Use Only* telegram on the foreign exchange problems of Italy in the bathroom of a Rome hotel where, because of an intestinal upset, he had been spending much time. He missed it only after he was on his way back to Paris. He did not report it, and for weeks he worried lest it should be discovered and traced to his carelessness. His bag contained only the most recent issue of the *Foreign Service Journal* and the Department of State *Newsletter* and some Congressional Hearings. The *Journal* reproduced a note from twenty-five years earlier saying that Ellis Briggs had been assigned as First Secretary to Lima, warned that morale in the Foreign Service was still declining and carried a lengthy article, "The New Role of the Agricultural Attaché," by a man named Luther Mendel Burbank. The Department of State *Newsletter* was not greatly more promising. It featured a front-page picture of Pethwick presenting a twenty-five-year-service award to his driver in Flores the previous May. Pethwick had spoken warmly of his loyalty. No mention was made of the highly unreliable information on the actual and intended movements of the American Ambassador which he had been providing to the Martínez police for all of this period. Others would have provided it. They might have been less adept on the Puerto Santos roads. So, sensibly, he had been kept on.

The pilot broke in to say that they were passing Princeton, "the birthplace of Woodrow Wilson," and would be

soon crossing the Delaware. He went on to say that Phil-
adelphia, birthplace of Benjamin Franklin and headquarters of the Duponts, would soon be visible to those
on the right side of the cabin. The stream of misinforma-
tion continued. Campbell abandoned his intention to
read and settled down to reflect on the day. They were
influential men; clearly they had appreciated what he
had to say; it was good that they now had the full picture.
Campbell did not stop to consider on whom they had influence. Not on the Senators from New York. These were
liberals and not, unhappily, the kind whom the yearning
for respectability makes decently susceptible to the established view. Not the Congressmen; they were far too ple-
beian even to hope for notice by members of the Council.
Not the *New York Times* or the *Post*; it was their influence
he was seeking to offset. His audience did not, as Marxists
would imagine, control banks or investments in Puerto
Santos. Since United Fruit pulled out and Martínez had
moved in, foreign investment had been negligible. Influence is evidently a rather subjective thing; in foreign
affairs a man is influential if he so regards himself. But
influence does have a practical aspect. Various of the
men to whom Worth Campbell had just spoken, because
they were influential, spoke regularly to the Secretary and
to the President. Or they were consulted. On such occasions they might now mention their concern about possible Communist penetration in Puerto Santos or their sat-
isfaction that it was being competently watched. While
Worth Campbell did not reflect on the sources of his audience's influence, he thought briefly of this latter fact.

13

Sr. Andrés Medina Alvárez was not the first of his name and family to serve his country on an important mission abroad. A distant ancestor had set out for England on behalf of Philip II and the Holy Faith in the year 1588. That mission had something in common with his. The strategic situation was unfavorable. The country to which he was sent had been subject to much hostile propaganda, and it has even been argued that ardent Catholicism and militant Communism arouse the same adverse reaction. The odds in both instances were unfavorable. The first Medina never reached his destination; his defeat, largely attributable to superior British naval power, had ever since been blamed on God, partly in order to relieve Spanish arms of the responsibility for its errors and partly to prove that Englishmen could accept the Reformation without divine retribution. All of this was known to the Finance Minister. It might have provided grounds for reflection except that he was tired, and on the plane up from Miami he was forced to share seats with a young woman whose virtue, he concluded, was protected only by her slatternly dress and obvious unwillingness to bathe. She held with indifference a deeply aggrieved and very moist child. So he had confined himself to waiting for the time to pass and wondering if American advertising no longer warned against body odor and halitosis. He was sorry that he had made a point of traveling tourist class, and he missed the small thrill of excitement he had always earlier experienced on entering the United States.

He was met at Friendship Airport in Baltimore by the Representative that Miró had dispatched to Washington immediately after the revolution and his wife, and nothing that happened thereafter had improved the Minister's spirits. On the drive to Washington the Representative had described in detail, and with no slight exaggeration, his efforts to extract money and recognition since coming to the United States. All this, though with even greater exaggeration, he had previously reported to Flores. Franklin in Paris suffered by comparison. But Washington still viewed the Miró government like a case of the yaws. The Representative sometimes wondered if Madera and Ryan were worth the price. Currently there was much concern about Miró's plans for the Martínez properties. He outlined a number of highly improbable plots by unemployed Martínez friends and relatives against their country and guessed that they were using money freely on Capitol Hill. It was known they had bought one of the news magazines and possibly *The Wall Street Journal*. The Representative's wife said they couldn't manage on the money they were getting — even the Haitian ambas-

sador had more. The Minister derived a moment's satis-
faction from deciding that she should continue to suffer.

More depressing still, the Representative reported that
during the afternoon an aide of Assistant Secretary of
State Grant Worthing Campbell had telephoned to say
that his principal, with whom the round of talks should,
at a minimum, begin, would be tied up all day tomorrow.
He had asked if the Minister would wish to see Mr. Symes
Jones. Mr. Jones was the Assistant Secretary's deputy
and was well informed. That had been left open. Finally,
there was an urgent, strictly personal message for the
Minister from Flores from the President; this was being
held for safekeeping at the Embassy. The Representative
had, in fact, read it himself. He thought it only his duty to
keep informed.

•

Assistant Secretary Campbell had a reasonably good
excuse for not seeing the Minister next day. Apart from
indicating that the United States, or in any case the
United States as personified by Grant Worthing Campbell, viewed the Miró regime with, as it was officially
termed, "reserve," he had in these closing days of the Congress to brief the House Foreign Affairs Committee on
Latin American matters. Since it was the last crisis in
the area, this meant considerable attention to Puerto
Santos.

It was a necessary chore, although neither the Senate
Foreign Relations Committee nor the House Foreign Affairs Committee any longer has much power. The fault

lies largely with the chairmen and ranking members. In the past, these have often been disagreeable and vituperative men. Public officials, even Secretaries of State, will make prudent concessions to a mean and cantankerous legislator in order to forestall demands that he — the official or Secretary — be ousted, publicly scourged for misfeasance, hauled into court as a traitor or be subject to legislation making him answerable in all of his actions to Mr. J. Edgar Hoover. Meanness makes greatly for influence. In more recent times the chairmen and senior members have been gentlemen and, accordingly, no appeasement has been called for. So they have been without influence. The Senate Committee still retains some of the prestige derived from the unique nastiness, and hence the power, of its past leaders. The House Committee lacks even that.

On the day of the postponed appointment with the Finance Minister of Puerto Santos, there was not even a very good attendance at the huge green and mahogany table around which the members of the House Committee and the witnesses sit in companionable proximity. One Democrat appears only when Israel and the Arabs are under discussion. He naturally was absent. So was a Republican who for eighteen years had specialized exclusively on the question of the recognition of Red China which he opposes. Yet others had anticipated adjournment and departed on inspection trips to Paris, Rome, London, Madrid, Miami and other centers of strategic American interest. Of those that remained, one was uncertain of the location of Puerto Santos. This was settled with the assistance of a map at which he continued to gaze with greatly aroused interest. Another was under the impression that the Communist take-over had already occurred. Before the Assistant Secretary had finished persuading him to the contrary, he got up and left, angry and obviously unconvinced.

None of this was unduly disconcerting to Worth Campbell. He was an old hand. But it did remind him to put the Puerto Santos problem in rather categorical terms. Accordingly, he stressed the commitment of the United States to orderly and progressive democracy in Latin America. He made clear our concern that this be genuine democracy and not a cover for a Communist take-over. It was our policy to stand firm, at all points, against the Communist conspiracy. To yield would be fatal, as experience had so often shown. Noting that they were in executive session, he restated rather frankly his misgivings about some of the men in Puerto Santos. In Czechoslovakia, Poland, Hungary, Bulgaria, Albania, control of the police had been vital in achieving Communist power. Control of education had been vital in consolidating it. Events in Puerto Santos were in the same pattern. Could Miró control them? It remained to be seen. Until he showed that he could, he could expect no help from the United States. And, as at the Council, he implied that Miró might already be hurting for such help. The Committee was perhaps aware that his Finance Minister was even now in Washington.

The first questions as usual were perfunctory. They came from the senior members. It is not that they take foreign policy crises in stride. But there are few countries in the Americas — Canada and perhaps Costa Rica apart — where in the past fifteen years the Committee has not been warned of dangerous developments. So also in Africa. And likewise in the Middle East and the rest of Asia. In these circumstances alarm does not remain at the same high tension as in the Council of Foreign Relations. To the older statesmen the warnings have a slightly ritualistic quality rather like those of eternal damnation in the Episcopal service.

However, eventually the questioning came to two young Congressmen at the end of the table. The Assistant Secretary had noticed them early in the hearing. Evidently beneficiaries of the Goldwater debacle — Campbell found himself thinking of them as temporary — one had been watching the Assistant Secretary with an annoying and possibly skeptical smile. Twice, at least, he had leaned over to his companion and made some remark, evidently about Campbell's testimony, to which the other had responded with a wide grin.

Worth Campbell knew that he was not without a sense of humor. No man in his position could survive without it. But he did not tolerate irresponsibility in himself or others. Once at a Christmas party at his Institute the students had put on a skit featuring the life of Worth Campbell. Much of it was harmless. He was visibly amused by one scene in which, as the ghost of Senator John Sherman, he was shown threatening the despairing tycoons of the Ruhr with the American antitrust laws. But he had deeply resented the very first scene which had shown his mother, just prior to his birth, being frightened by a wolf which bore the mustache and facial expression of Joseph Stalin. This was no laughing matter; the fate of civilization was involved. The people who had planned the evening's merriment had noticed with no small pleasure that here their Director did not smile.

Now one of the young Congressmen cleared his throat and said: "Mr. Secretary. Don't you think there is danger in carrying these historical analogies too far? Did you think that President Kennedy was planning a left wing take-over when he put his brother Edward in charge of the Department of Justice and the FBI?"

The Assistant Secretary was almost too genial in his reply. "I think, Congressman, our traditions are a little different from those of a Latin American republic. Might I add that I think you have the wrong Kennedy."

There was a ripple of laughter in Campbell's favor, but the Congressman was unperturbed: "I'm sorry. Some would say they are interchangeable. But why if these analogies are unwise do you say there is one between Puerto Santos and Czechoslovakia?"

"For the simple reason," the Assistant Secretary said, "that the Communist Party was, and is, in full operation in both places. And we believe it to have the same goals in both places." Again it was clear from the general reaction that Worth Campbell had scored. But the fellow was persistent. Like so many Congressmen, once possessed of a certain amount of information he was determined to make the most of it.

"Can we say that Communist goals are always the

same, Mr. Secretary? I take it that Khrushchev did not approve of Stalin's goals. And the Chinese do not approve
of the goals of the Russians. And in China the Maoist
cultural revolution seems to have one set of goals and the
other Chinese another. And right now the Russians and
the Chinese do not seem to think Fidel Castro has any
goals. How about that?"

It was now clear that the fellow was trying to be clever.
In spite of himself, Worth Campbell was beginning to
lose patience. He dropped any pretense of geniality from
his voice and replied, "I think you know, Congressman,
or should, that whatever the disagreements between the
Communists they are united in their intention to destroy
the free world."

The two had indeed arranged matters, for his colleague now took up the questioning. "When you say, Mr.
Secretary, that we must always stand absolutely firm, that
any retreat will be exploited, I wonder if you would criti-
cize our government's policy during the Cuban missile
crisis? As I remember it, both we and the Russians gave
way a bit. Both were greatly praised for doing so."

"I think the history shows that it was principally the
Russians that gave way." Worth Campbell could feel
himself getting quite angry. It was time for real self-control.

"Well, did that lead *them* into an endless series of re-
treats of the kind you fear?"

Campbell's voice developed a marked edge. "Congressman, I am here this morning to discuss the policies
of the United States and not those of the Soviet Union."

He was being baited, and he sensed that he was not handling it well. Soon would come a question about Puerto Santos, and, his earlier answers having been defensive, he would not carry conviction on this. The Committee room, moreover, had come out of its accustomed torpor. Members who previously had been gazing at the ceiling were now looking at Worth Campbell. Two members of the minority who had been reminiscing competitively on past political campaigns reluctantly paused to listen. Around the edge of the room on tilted chairs and at heavily littered desks in the corners were the Committee clerks. Previously they had been only simulating attention. Such store does our culture set by useful toil that not even the employees of a Congressional Committee can afford to seem totally idle. Now instead of seeming to listen, they were paying attention.

"I appreciate that our concern today is with Puerto Santos," said the second Congressman. "And I know how deeply you and the Secretary of State are concerned about the danger of another Munich. But even if, as you say, the Communists are not divided, they do seem a trifle confused. So I wonder if this isn't the time to show a little flexibility. I read in the papers that this fellow Miró is a very decent fellow who is trying to do a job on education and economic development and things like that and that he has taken steps to get rid of the police state. Couldn't we just run a few risks and give him a hand?"

A man from the office of the Assistant Secretary of State for Congressional Relations had come to the session with Campbell. His responsibilities were not great. Like the Committee clerks', they principally consisted in seeming to be paying attention. But in addition he had to pass to the Assistant Secretary a slip of paper bearing the name and state of any Congressman who entered the discussion. During the long question, Worth Campbell looked at the slip. He saw the word Missouri.

"I would hope, Congressman, you might be open to evidence other than mine. You have mentioned education. It happens that we have just had a report on education in Puerto Santos under the new regime. It is not by one of my fellow bureaucrats but by one of the best known and most distinguished professional educators from your own state. I see no reason at the moment, Mr. Chairman, why it shouldn't go into the record, although as a matter of courtesy I should check before releasing the author's name. Let me read a little of what this distinguished educator says about education in Puerto Santos, including its use for personal propaganda by the present Minister of Education."

•

The hearing ended with thanks to the Assistant Secretary. He shook hands with the Chairman and walked out into the busy corridors of the Capitol with the ranking minority member, a friend since the Marshall Plan days and the 80th Congress. Worth Campbell declined his invitation to lunch, pleading work, and they walked together down to the portico to his car. Others were waiting on the steps. The Capitol Plaza was golden in the high autumn sun. "You came down pretty hard on our young friend," said the Congressman. "Lucky you had that report with you. That was real news. I think the American people should know about it."

"I can't release it — an executive session. I try to live by the rules."

"So do I except where the public interest is involved."

14

BACK AT HIS OFFICE Worth Campbell found Symes Jones waiting to ask him how it went. Worth Campbell said fine, feeling slightly less than sure, and learned that the Finance Minister had sent a courteous note saying that he would not take up the Deputy Assistant Secretary's time but would await the convenience of the Assistant Secretary who, he realized, was a very busy man. Campbell settled down to the stack of telegrams and messages on his desk. On top was a long telegram from Joe Hurd. It was, Joe said, additional background for the Finance Minister's visit.

When his feelings were engaged, Hurd tended to forget the established rules of diplomatic communication — the passive voice, avoidance of idiom, no unqualified conclusions, well-considered ambiguity, all sentences to begin with "It." Now he began well, but his concluding sentences were careless. "Unless we move fast the generals are going to throw Miró out. Instead of someone who is trying to do a job, we will probably have another old-fashioned military dictatorship down here."

Two more messages concerned Puerto Santos. One was on Department stationery from Pethwick. It said: "I have seen the telegram from the Chargé in Puerto Santos. It cannot be accepted as a sound statement of the situation, and it cannot be accepted as a sound view of the American and free world interest in that country. Its view of Miró is especially unsound and unduly uncritical. It was my experience with Mr. Hurd that his judgment was often not entirely reliable during my service there as Ambassador." The other message was sealed, and Campbell recognized it as an emergency appreciation from CIA.

Its language was as formal as Joe Hurd's was careless — highly compressed telegraphese that stopped just short of being impenetrable. It also said that Miró was in trouble. It gave, as an intelligence estimate, that only restoration of full diplomatic relations and prompt assistance could keep him in office. It avoided any suggestions as to the proper course of action. It did, however, offer the further estimate that the alternative to Miró would be a military government and that its policies would be less in keeping with the avowed aims of American policy than those of the present administration. While Campbell was still deciphering this dispatch, his secretary buzzed to say that the Secretary of Defense was calling on the phone.

The Washington protocol that requires the lesser of two officials to get on the line and await the pleasure of his superior in rank is, on the whole, more binding than any legislation enacted by the Medes, the Persians or the combined empire of the two. And it is enforced not by the illiterate and often incompetent police of those states, but by highly skilled secretaries who can call to mind, with a speed and accuracy unapproached by any computer, the most minute gradations in official precedence. They have reason. Their own position on the Washington ladder is derived from that of their employer. All abhorred the Secretary of Defense who remained on the wire while his secretary dialed and sometimes dialed himself. His belief that this was more efficient was a menace to the entire social structure.

He was now on the wire and said: "Hello, Worth. We've got an interesting communication in this morning from the young fellow we left behind in Puerto Santos when we pulled out our people. His name is González, and he knows the language, and our people say he is fairly bright. He thinks we should recognize the Miró Administration down there and give them substantial aid. If we don't, he says the generals will take over."

Worth Campbell had a little time while the Secretary was speaking both to size up the situation and decide his own reaction — but not much.

"I think our boys must be getting together down there, Mr. Secretary. This is the third message in almost exactly the same language that has come into my office in the last fifteen minutes."

"Well, I wanted you to know about it, and I don't trust channels. The amount of paper that moves these days. My people thought it was interesting, and it isn't too often that one of our soldiers comes out on the liberal side of an argument."

Campbell had by now collected his ideas. "We've got some things to worry about down there, Mr. Secretary. We left a fairly young and inexperienced team behind when we pulled out the Ambassador and the rest. I'd like to go into the full story with you sometime."

"Any time at all. We just thought this lad's signal was interesting. I'll stand by for your call." In Washington to say that you will stand by for a call is to mean that the matter is not to be discussed further.

They might have been a little smarter, Campbell reflected as he put the telephone back on the console. They could have spaced the messages a day or two apart. Or varied the predictions a bit. He had often noticed that when a man had a blind spot on one subject he was likely to be pretty naïve in his general reaction. Nonetheless, the telegrams from these youngsters would cause him some trouble. They would encourage the wrong people. He reminded himself not to speak of them as youngsters. It put younger men off, and Joe Hurd was old enough to know better — as old as he was himself, he guessed.

*

During the day the Puerto Santos Finance Minister had another depressing talk with their Representative. Then things brightened, for the Ambassador to the OAS called and asked him to his house in Georgetown for drinks and a bite of dinner. They had known each other since the Bretton Woods Conference in 1944. Once the Ambassador, out of office under Eisenhower and on a trip, had stayed with him for several days in Flores. They had gone together by horseback to the cattle country in the mountains. He opened the street door himself when the Finance Minister arrived and led the way upstairs to a handsome, well-used living room which half-surrounded a lighted brick terrace and garden. An elderly retainer took orders for drinks and brought pieces of cheese and sliced carrots. They talked about earlier meetings, half-forgotten adventures. Finally the Ambassador brought the discussion around to the business at hand.

"You have friends here in town, but I'm afraid you must face it, they are not the most useful ones. In fact, you seem to have all the wrong ones. The youngsters in the White House are for you. But they are supposed to help the President and not conduct foreign policy, and to some extent they don't. The people down the line at State are sympathetic, but it's a great handicap being down the line. I think some AID people are sympathetic, but they are coordinated by Worth Campbell and that is the same as being down the line. Some of our intelligence people are for you, but they are supposed to hew to the official line. I am for you, but my age puts me pretty far down the line."

"You have, I gather, what is called a line organization," said the Finance Minister. "I assume your German allies now speak admiringly of the formality and discipline of the American bureaucracy. Why is there this unfortunate difficulty with the people at the top of the line, including Dr. Campbell?"

"Prudence and caution. They wish to be completely

sure that your government is not subject to unfriendly influences."

"By that they mean the Communists?"

"Yes, the Communists. Come, let us eat."

The two old men sat at one end of the big dining-room table. Both ate rather sparsely. Each recalled another incident or two associated with earlier encounters. The Minister asked what had become of Henry Morgenthau, Marriner Eccles, Milton Eisenhower, Tom Connally, Walter George, Leo Crowley, Lincoln Gordon and Henry Wallace. Then he returned to the subject that was on his mind.

"Do your friends think that my young President is a Communist? Or General Pérez? Or me? I have heard it said of Ryan, but he now spends his time teaching the alphabet to our infants. That is surely a harmless occupation for a revolutionary."

"You must not confuse fear of Communists with their existence. I have been around this city for forty years, and I am not at all sure that the two are much related."

"But why are our young men feared? You must excuse me if I persist. You will understand why."

"Your young men, as you call them, are not feared. What is feared is the consequences of misjudging them. Nothing in our government counts so badly against a man as misjudging someone who turns out to be a Communist. The retribution is unmerciful. Fear of being wrong immobilizes both thought and action. I sometimes think the Communists worked it out themselves — first they learned to wash the brain and then to freeze it."

"The world does get very complicated," said the Finance Minister. "Tell me, what do you advise?"

"You must hope for the best and then try to see the President."

"Can that be arranged?"

"Frankly, I doubt it."

The conversation drifted back to Roosevelt.

•

When it came time to go back to the Embassy where he was staying, the Finance Minister refused the Ambassador's offer to call a cab. (He had earlier declined an offer of the Representative's car and a suggestion that a car and driver be hired for his stay. It would have been convenient and the expense inconsequential, but he knew that his economy would add to the suffering of the Representative's wife. It was increasingly evident that she was a silly bitch.) It was turning cold; but the distance was not great, and the Minister knew he would enjoy the walk.

To one accustomed to the shabbiness and decay of a South American city, the untidiness of tropical vegetation and the unkempt habits of the very poor, Washington always seemed unbelievably splendid. The tidy, well-pruned trees, brick and fresh paint and high flat facades of Georgetown, varied yet in larger harmony, looked especially elegant to the Minister tonight. For the first time since he arrived, he was almost happy. He also knew the reason and warned himself accordingly. The Americans didn't put the public business in the hands of kindly, generous idealistic men like the old friend he had just left. Tougher, more disillusioned men less open to ideas and persuasion were used to wield the real power. "Hard-nosed was the modern word; he knew it well from the Latin American edition of *Time* which judged men in accordance with whether they were adequately hard-nosed. But however indispensable they might be for sound judgment and firm decision, such men were rather nasty. This the Americans realized. So they always had some agreeable and reasonable men around to take the sharp edge off life. Thus they partly redeemed themselves.

However, the Minister did not fool himself. He knew that his real work would be with the hard-nosed men.

•

Mrs. Kent had not been well. She was mildly arthritic and critically homesick for Columbia, Missouri, and in spite of her husband's urging rarely stirred out of their small, neat, rather Spartan apartment in Arlington. Television had become her principal comfort. What he called Mrs. Kent's condition had been one of Dr. Kent's reasons for wanting to get back to Washington.

"What was on the news?" He asked the familiar question as he slid into the small table in the dinette. He made a point of keeping up her interest in things.

"One of the President's little dogs is sick."

"Anything else?"

"Nothing. Speech by Nixon. Oh yes, I almost forgot. They have uncovered a Communist plot in that place you just were. Puerto Santos."

"A Communist plot? What happened?"

"It was to take over the educational system. It came out at a hearing here in Washington today."

"That is very important. Did they say any more?"

"It seems someone from here has just been down there and uncovered the whole thing."

Mrs. Kent's eyes glistened as he told her whose report it almost certainly was. She was sure, though, that they hadn't mentioned his name; she would have noticed it. They did say the report had been secret.

There was brief further mention of the report, although not of its author, on later newscasts. They had it pretty nearly right considering the abbreviation. In the course of the evening Dr. Kent decided he was just as happy to be anonymous. He had thought of Whittaker Chambers and the Pumpkin Papers and all that that led to.

15

AT SOME POINT in the weeks following the fall of Martínez, it had occurred to Worth Campbell that he should
get a little information on the ex-Dictator's son. He had
nothing very specific in mind. Campbell was an experienced man, and he knew that while the United States, in
its relations with lesser and dependent powers, can often
break a politician, it can rarely if ever make one. And
few things pay off as badly for those involved as an abor-
tive attempt at such manufacture. The failed Warwick
gets no credit for a good try; he is simply a man who tries
foolish things.

Yet Campbell sensed that if the threat to the free world
that was posed by Madera and Ryan and more subtly by
Aragón was to be contained, there would have, one day,
to be an alternative to Miró. It was not enough to keep
on saying that alternatives were always available in Latin
America. One needed on occasion to name names. The
old generals were not ideal. The *Alianza* had proclaimed
itself against military dictatorships. However unpractical

or out of keeping with the Latin need for discipline, this was still a commitment. So any return to open military rule had to be discouraged.

Young Martínez was a civilian. Any open move in his direction would of course arouse the more emotional liberals. It would have, at least momentarily, a bad press. Perhaps these objections would prove decisive. But on the other side the old Martínez allies and retainers on Capitol Hill would be pleased, and they were still a force to be reckoned with. And there was no escaping the fact that he was a member of a family that had given the country more than three decades of stable, solidly non-Communist rule. In Nicaragua, the Somozas, first the old general and then the sons, had served extremely well. Perhaps it was young Martínez's picture in the paper on the day but one after the revolution that had put these thoughts in Worth Campbell's mind. Except for a passing mention to Symes Jones, he had not discussed them with anyone. He did not expect them to lead anywhere, but at least one could be informed.

Some men move from one set of friends to another as life and their career passes them along. Some, more stalwart, adhere even with effort to the friends of the past. Worth Campbell was one of the latter. He called his old friends when they did not call him. Official occasions apart, they provided much of his social life. One evening while dining at one of Washington's newly fashionable French restaurants called Les Deux Escargots with yet another prosperous old friend — also now in private law practice — from the days of Berlin and Lucius Clay, he saw at the next table the former Puerto Santos Ambassador. The latter was with a sleek, dark-haired much younger man who presently rose, shook hands affectionately with the old Ambassador, received an *abrazo* in return, looked with alarm at his watch, and hurried away. Worth Campbell excused himself and joined the Ambassador for a moment. After some perfunctory references to health he asked the Ambassador if he knew young Martínez. The Ambassador responded with enthusiasm — a fine hard-working boy, a true scholar, in every respect like his father and, as Americans would say, the apple of his daddy's eye. A worthy member of a fine family. He added that he had seen almost nothing of young Martínez himself, but there were many in Puerto Santos who knew him well. General Pérez, in spite of having gone over to Miró, was a good man and was, he thought, his godfather. He would, of course, make further inquiries and immediately inform the Secretary. He would also like to ask the Secretary if a man of his own experience could not be used in the Inter-American Bank or the World Bank or the International Monetary Fund. He wanted to continue to serve mankind.

Worth Campbell was a trifle perturbed and moved quickly to cool the Ambassador's enthusiasm. He doubted that there was any need to make inquiries in Flores; it was only that he had a natural interest in any young Latin Americans studying in the United States and especially one of such prominence. He elected to ignore the Ambassador's plea for employment, as he had previously ignored what was probably meant to be a knowing wink. To cover himself, Campbell next day put a note in the files on the conversation stressing the limited nature of his interest. He had thought no more of the encounter, but it had reminded him to write yet another old friend from Berlin days who was now a professor of international relations at the University of Michigan. The response was with the day's stack of papers and telegrams on the day after the hearing before the House Foreign Affairs Committee. He came to it halfway through the pile.

> You were very wise to inquire informally. This draft question and the fuss over the people at Michigan State working for CIA has made everyone around here very sensitive to inquiries on student or, for that matter, any sort of collaboration with the government. Some of my colleagues even shy away from giving information on students and other professors to the FBI. . . .
>
> As to young Martínez he has made comparatively little impression on the campus, but he seems to have been quite constructive. He takes his classes quite seriously and does better than average work though the people I have talked with share my impression that he is very quiet. I have heard that he gets involved in student activities and discussions of a fairly high level, in a quiet way, but I have no first-hand information on this. Students these days usually have pretty impractical views as you know, but that was probably always so. I suppose you were a radical in your day. He takes no part in athletics . . .

The Assistant Secretary's secretary came into the dark-paneled office. Like those of the Secretary and Under

Secretary upstairs, it also suggested a serious overproduction of plywood. She sidled skillfully through the nearly closed door; it is a mode of entry known to all good Washington secretaries, for it means that the interior of the office is never suddenly exposed by a yawning gap to the world outside. She was especially well-trained. Once years before when she still worked at Commerce, she had opened a door wide to announce that people had arrived for a meeting. All assembled had seen the acting head of the Bureau of Foreign and Domestic Commerce stroking, among other things, the bare bottom of a lady editor of *The Statistical Abstract*. The memory still haunted her.

"Mr. Secretary, your ten-fifty-five appointment is here."

"I will come out and meet the Minister."

.

The sun, as it usually seemed to do, poured into the Executive Dining Room on the top floor. Bill O'Donnell was having lunch with a friend and, it might truthfully be said, a co-conspirator from the White House. It was the former academic assistant of Worth Campbell. They were not at the central table but at a smaller one for two at the side. There are two schools of thought in Washington about lunching with journalists and those with whom one is concerting action against superiors. Some believe in a club, a very discreet restaurant or the privacy of your office. Others say that even in the most cautiously chosen location the wrong man walks by the table, observes the conversation thoughtfully from a distance or, being your superior, walks into the office without knocking. The circumstances being suspect, all suspect the worst. Better disarm suspicion by doing everything in public. Such was the O'Donnell doctrine although, in practice, it was not carried to the extremes of having lunch with anyone working for Drew Pearson. There was some additional protection in the present instance for both men were proceeding to a common meeting.

The dining room was not crowded. Difficult as it may be for the outsider to imagine, there are periods of considerable tranquillity in American foreign policy. It remains necessary, nonetheless, that all the world be covered; an eye must be kept on Cyprus and Ceylon and on around the world to Panama. A railway gateman is no less necessary because no train is coming. But neither is he overworked. Such in these particular days was the general state of idleness that many felt the need to conceal it by remaining at their desks. It was a time when reports on economic conditions in the Bombay consular area, on civil disturbances in the Shan states, on the long-range plans for solving the water problems in Hong Kong, and on the accomplishments of the United States Delegation to UNESCO were being rather carefully read.

"Could you get him in to see the President?" Bill O'Donnell asked.

"No." His companion had learned that there was sometimes emphasis in extreme brevity. And being at the White House, he had also learned, reduced the need to justify and explain.

"Then we might as well write him off and Miró too. He sure as hell isn't going to get anything out of Campbell."

"Platespecialyousa. Platespecialoutonionsyousa." The waitress had materialized beside the table, brought a plate down in front of each with emphasis, brought a piece of paper from the pocket of her uniform for momentary examination an inch or two from her glasses, pivoted and departed. In color, design and arrangement — half-toasted roll, cap of very brown meat, slight ooze of gravy, thin slice of red tomato, curled sheet of light green lettuce — each plate resembled an advertisement of Swift & Company on the heavily coated color pages of a woman's magazine. It was, perhaps, a trifle less appetizing. Neither man paid it much attention.

"What happened this morning?"

"I kept the notes for the memorandum of conversation. It will be concise, almost literate and to the point; I am sorry no one will ever read it. How fortunate the files! My Assistant Secretary was, as always, exceedingly polite and courteous. If he didn't squint like a turtle through those shitty little glasses, he would, I believe, be called urbane. In addition, he was friendly though not affable, a shade condescending and very, very negative. I was reminded of a meeting between Senator J. William Fulbright and Marshal Nguyen Cao Ky."

"I have heard we should be more concerned with the substance of our diplomacy, less with the style."

"Ah, yes. The unfailing mark of the amateur. Well, there was plenty of substance, all familiar, all bad. We give aid not as an obligation or an act of charity or because we want to be liked. We give it because we are deeply concerned about the preservation of democracy and the security of the free world. And we are concerned because your government seems to be dominated by a couple of fucking Reds — I believe he just said men about whom we have reason to be uncertain. So much for the Minister of Interior and Minister of Education. As long as they are there, no dice. More specifically, no dough. Nor any assurance on the sugar quota. We would be especially reluctant to give any arms to a government we did not completely trust."

"How did what's-his-name take it?"

"He is a very stalwart old citizen, I concluded. He said that Miró and Madera were not Communists, and that Madera and Ryan were the two most popular members of the Administration and had the best reputation for getting things done. Without them who would Miró have? Answer: Nobody who would appeal to the people, and after all these years the people wanted some action. Men like himself could be sacrificed, but not those the people liked. Also if they went, Miró would have to rely completely on the generals. It is, perhaps, no secret that they are not his strongest supporters. He barely hinted that there might also be adverse effects from yielding to Yankee pressure — as it could be called. He was very tactful."

"How did Campbell react? Your food is getting cold."

"I would say that Dr. Campbell was imperturbable. Anyhow, he was trying to look imperturbable, and he did it well. He noticed that the old man had omitted to underwrite Ryan's political affiliations and let it be noticed that he had noticed this oversight. And very politely he brought up this business of Ryan using his Ministry to build a personal propaganda machine — the thing that was in the papers this morning from that old bastard in AID. In a matter of moments millions of little Marxists will be running in and out of the canebrakes. Very irresponsible. The Minister, I gathered, had not foreseen this disaster and could only say it was unlikely. Then they got on to the Martínez properties."

"That's whether they should be nationalized?"

"Not exactly. Medina said they had been badly managed — which is true — and getting worse. Miró wants to take over any land that can be divided up and give it to the peasants as he promised. The rest, including the big sugar and coffee operations, he wants to sell to get some of the money he needs. Similarly the business concerns and the city real estate. Does that sound reasonable?"

"Yes."

"Well, it isn't. And when you get tired of the affection of those who love you for your influence on the President, I advise you to go back to teaching. Your mind isn't subtle enough for this city. In the *Alianza* we are broadly committed to economic development under private enterprise. We seek to build confidence, encourage the flow of private capital. If you start seizing private land and property, what would David Rockefeller say? What would Keith Funston say? What, in particular, would Senator Bourke B. Hickenlooper say? Do you understand the Hickenlooper Amendment?"

"Not especially."

"Here I feel a certain sympathy. This morning I was confused myself. But, in a word, the Hickenlooper Amendment cuts off aid to countries nationalizing American-owned property without compensation. It seems that just before or just after he was heaved, Martínez deeded all of his Puerto Santos property, meaning most of the country, to his son. This affluent lad lives in Ann Arbor, Michigan. He isn't an American citizen but, as a bona fide American resident, he comes under the protection of American law."

"Look, this strikes me as crazy." By now the White House visitor sounded a little impatient, a little tired of O'Donnell's mocking voice. "Let's get this straight. Didn't Martínez get his property by theft, forced sale, larceny or whatever you call it?"

"The business about the Hickenlooper Amendment is, I think, a large pile of horse-shit. And Campbell probably knows it is. Its application to bona fide residents, so-called, is something some genius in the Legal Adviser's Office came up with possibly on instructions. Lawyers are like that. In fact the fellow was there this morning, and I thought he looked ashamed. But Medina didn't knows it is. Its application to bona fide residents, so-Campbell feels it is legitimate to use any available argument against action he knows to be unwise and un-American. As a matter of practical procedure you don't fight fire with fire, but you do fight error with untruth. As to your point about the property being stolen, naturally Medina brought that up."

"What did Campbell say?"

"Gentle, brilliant and on this, especially condescending. 'I have heard it said that the methods by which some of our great industrial families acquired their wealth would not bear too much examination. But we couldn't for that reason now take over the property of the Rockefellers, the Mellons, the Guggenheims, Averell Harriman, Jock Whitney, Joseph P. Kennedy.' Pretty persuasive, don't you think? Medina looked quite discouraged."

"I think he should see the President."

"How do we go about it?"

"I'll speak to the Vice-President. I think the Justice might put in a word. Maybe we can get some help from one or two of the other boys in the White House. A call from Wayne Morse wouldn't hurt. Possibly a word from the Ambassador would be useful — didn't he have your friend Medina to dinner last night? We mustn't overdo it. Have your friend write the President a personal letter outlining the situation and asking for his personal consideration."

"It would be in accordance with emergency protocol and probably more effective if I wrote it for him myself. Any suggestions as to what it should say?"

"Well, stress convergence of two great traditions in the United States and Puerto Santos. Washington, Jefferson, Lincoln, Roosevelt, the President; Cortés, Pizarro, San Martin, Bolívar, Miró. Each country now has the culminating leader. But don't overdo it. Maybe you better leave out Pizarro. Don't you want your dessert?"

•

Late that afternoon the Finance Minister had the first encouraging news since arriving in Washington. The Representative came into the small office that he was using in the Chancery of the Puerto Santos Embassy.

"Excellency, I have important word for you. I have just talked with Mr. O'Donnell in the State Department. I think we are going to be able to arrange for us to see the President."

·

The office of the President of the United States is one of great power. All but the most lackadaisical and inarticulate members of the White House press corps at least once during their lives write a book about it and its relation to the Washington press. Beginning at the same point, and proceeding with a similar desire to do as much as possible for their profession, all reach the same three conclusions. The first is that the White House press has great responsibilities because the President has great responsibilities. The second is that the White House press has great power because the President has great power. The third is that the President should hold more frequent press conferences. Not enough attention has been paid in this excellent and predictable work to the power of Grant Worthing Campbell. Over the whole range of matters affecting the life and death of man it is infinitely less than that of the President. But on the very specific matters with which Campbell is concerned, it can be much greater. Puerto Santos was such a specific matter. Accordingly a contest of wills between the President of the

United States and his Assistant Secretary of State for Inter-American Affairs and Coordinator of the Alliance for Progress is not at all unequal. There can be such a contest without anyone knowing it.

Two days after his meeting with Sr. Medina, the Assistant Secretary, on returning to his office from the barber shop, got a message relaying a telephone call from his former assistant. The latter was just on the point of leaving town with the President. The message had been typed out by Campbell's secretary, read back to the White House secretary and was as follows:

> The President had a fairly long meeting this afternoon with the Puerto Santos Finance Minister. The President was very much impressed by what the Minister said about Miró, and his efforts to establish stable government and make up for some of the lost time under Martínez. Tell Dr. Campbell that I was there myself, and it was a fairly impressive presentation. The President would like to have a fairly thorough review of our policy to see if we shouldn't extend full recognition and substantial aid to Miró. The President was particularly concerned that if Miró falls we might get another military dictatorship down there. He would like something on this in the next day or two.

The man from the White House had allowed his sympathies slightly to improve on his assigned role as a bloodless adjutant. The meeting had not been especially lengthy, but there was no harm in implying presidential interest and involvement. The words "fairly impressive" describing the Minister's presentation could have been an overstatement. The old man was too eager, too anxious to reassure, in fact, a little desperate. The President had not suggested any time limit for the review; to invoke one was standard practice for all Executive departments and *de rigeur* for the Department of State. Recognition and aid had at best been only distantly implied. In point of fact, after the meeting had broken up, the President had said: "Get on to those fellows over there and find out what they are thinking. I don't want to get credit for another military dictatorship down there."

16

THE HISTORY AS ALSO THE LITERATURE of diplomacy has greatly celebrated its association with sex. Many of its more breathtaking accomplishments have been initiated, or on occasion completed, in bed. A hundred years and more ago this was probable, for as always deeper social forces explain the frivolous. Diplomats then were not terribly busy; they had energy to spare. More important in a democracy, rulers are answerable to the people. They cannot, accordingly, be answerable to a woman. Despotisms, in contrast, were answerable to despots which meant they could be answerable to their wives or mistresses. This being so, diplomats, in line of duty, sought out the relevant woman and, if qualified, took her to bed.

The notion that diplomacy has a special identification with the bedroom has survived the fact. Historians have been partly responsible and novelists more so. They have sought to associate with their heroes a little of the wickedness the public rightly expects. There are few enough things that distinguish the modern ambassador from an electrical engineer.

In fact, the modern diplomat will not once in a long career encounter a woman he can functionally seduce and vice versa. He will also have been warned from his earliest days in the Service against women who might have his information as distinct from his other attributes primarily in mind. Known neglect of these warnings adversely affects the efficiency report on which hinges his career. So among the Americans on the Foreign Service roster in any overseas capital, there will be a normal amount of what, depending on age and rank, beginning with the Ambassador and the Class I officers and going down the grades, will be referred to as union of the sexes, sexual intercourse, making love, sleeping with, and, by the members of the Marine Guard with that special imagery which so often characterizes the speech of the untutored man, as "dipping the wick," and by the regional legal officer when he thinks of it as fornication. But all of this, the members of the Marine Guard excepted, will be at suitably regulated intervals with the individuals' lawful wives. That is why, in modern diplomatic history, nearly all of the transactions take place in an office. Truth may be as strange as fiction, but in diplomacy it is far less prurient. But in the more informal world of the intellect, the bedroom still has a role. So it had in Ann Arbor one Sunday morning in December. The sun was streaming into the room. During the course of the night, both occupants of the bed had discarded their night attire if, indeed, any had been worn.

The bedroom was in the rather old-fashioned fumed-oak

apartment house in Ann Arbor, Michigan. The girl with Juan César Martínez might still be recognized by a very few as the one who was so widely pictured in his arms on the day after the senior Martínez found refuge in the Paraguayan Embassy.

"I have something I must tell you, baby." It was Juan who spoke, and he turned a little to look at his partner.

"Goodness, the tone of voice. Are you pregnant?"

"Set your mind at rest, baby. Even you are not that accomplished. I am going home in a little while."

"I'm sorry. Does it mean you will be shot?"

"Not any more, it seems. It is now safe."

"When did you decide?"

"I've been thinking about it and that I should keep in touch. I don't want to stay here and teach, and I'm spoiled for the Riviera."

"You could go into politics."

"Not really. The Constitution says that you must be a natural-born American."

"That is a handicap if you want to be President. It must have been only a rumor that John Lindsay was born in Bethlehem. Does anyone know you are coming?"

"Quite a few have asked. A friend of my father's told me it would be a good idea. And there is a general in the new government who was my godfather. He has sent word I should come home. And Professor Schmiltz told me very confidentially that he had been asked, most confidentially, by the State Department if I might be interested in going home. Anyhow they asked about me. That was a surprise."

"I had a course last year from Schmiltz. He thinks he

is the greatest wheel in foreign affairs since Senator Van-
denberg. Georgie Hirsch says he is a Millimetternich, and
I think he is a boring little prick. When do you leave?"

"Over Christmas. As far as anyone knows it will just be
to visit my mother."

"I am glad you are nice to your mother. In spite of
everything she must have had problems. Can I go with
you?"

"No."

•

Juan Martínez had been candid but not completely
candid. In bed even non-diplomats often are not. With
the departure of his father he made the transition from
being the son of a South American dictator, which was
not much at the University of Michigan, to being the son
of an ex-dictator, which was even less. He had been
forced to face, with an urgency quite new in his experience, the question of what he was going to do. And, as he
had just said, everything, with astonishing force, pointed
back to Puerto Santos. Then he had received a letter from
an elderly Flores lawyer saying that shortly before his departure his father had called him in and executed a simple
will making his favorite and most presentable son the sole
heir to all his puerto Santos properties, the will to become
a deed of gift at any time that the old man retired from
office and left the country. Evidently his father, if he
hadn't seen the handwriting, had, at least, been looking
thoughtfully at the wall.

Juan had written back asking the old lawyer what would happen were he to return to Flores. The lawyer had asked none other than Madera himself who had replied that the new regime did not jail people for being related to Martínez. He did suggest that, were the boy to return, he should keep his nose clean, stay out of politics and, above all, keep clear of his old man's cronies in the army. The lawyer then asked General Pérez, a collaborator in many shady activities in earlier years. The general had forced his mind to move at an unusually rapid pace and said to tell the boy to come home. With some professional editing the lawyer had relayed this information to young Martínez. He had also told him not to count on owning his father's vast properties and thus the national wealth. The government had made clear its intention of taking them over and, it was said, was only waiting for full recognition by Washington before doing so.

•

Despite the injunctions to promptness, nearly ten days elapsed before Assistant Secretary Worth Campbell called a meeting to have a full-dress review of the Puerto Santos policy. There had been no deliberate delay; during the course of the week he had, in fact, warned the White House that the review would take a little time. The Secretary had just departed for the Middle East, Asia and Australia for meetings of SEATO, CENTO and ANZUS. He would not be back for four or five days. Worth Campbell also wanted to go over matters with his own staff. And he needed time to read and review the relevant papers. And he had his other responsibilities; Puerto Santos was not all of Latin America. At no time did it occur to the Assistant Secretary that his was the policy of the *status quo*, and this is admirably served by inaction. In Washington the President's word is Law. Still the White House contented itself with urging all possible speed.

Worth Campbell had another reason for proceeding with caution. The two Congressional Committees, the Council on Foreign Relations and numerous newsmen had been told by him that Miró was no bulwark against Communism. And they had been told that the United States feared that Madera and Ryan were bent on a Communist take-over. If the President now extended full recognition to Miró and gave him assistance, it would naturally be said that he was promoting such a take-over. No one could explain that on the assurance of an elderly and possibly senile Finance Minister the situation was suddenly safe. So the President was committed and not less so because it was by Campbell. The newspapers had naturally reported that Puerto Santos policy was being reexamined. A telephone call had already come from Worth Campbell's ranking minority friend on the Senate Foreign Relations Committee. "I thought you fellows were on to those Communists down there. Now I hear you are getting ready to help them. What the hell goes on?" A good public servant had not only a responsibility to his country and to the security of the free world; he must also protect his President from the criticism that is naturally aroused by any sharp break in established policy, any pulling back from such established commitments.

The day before the meeting Bill O'Donnell joined the Ambassador to the OAS for a drink at the Federal City Club to concert strategy. The Ambassador had a preference for circumspect as distinct from open conspiracy, and being of higher rank his wishes prevailed. The Federal City Club, a relatively recent foundation inhabited by Washington liberals, is a modest watering place consisting only of a bar and dining room. It was comparatively safe, for anyone concerned with foreign policy of sufficient importance to reflect intelligently on their meeting would belong to the Metropolitan Club. An exception, as it happened, was Worth Campbell who, because of past academic connections, was carried on the scholarly rolls of the Cosmos Club out beyond Dupont Circle. But Campbell was no threat. He dined only with old friends and drank only in line of duty. That evening, as it happened, he was celebrating some hundred and sixty years of independence, liberty and uninterrupted economic and social decline at the Haitian Embassy.

"What are the chances?" the Ambassador asked when they were seated and he had competently discouraged a friend from the National Gallery and an alcoholic news commentator from joining them.

"Which do you want, the view by which I sustain my morale or the harsh truth?"

"Suit yourself, but maybe you better tell me which it will be."

"You shall have the truth. Our Puerto Santos policy is, of course, wide open. Nothing will be settled until the meeting. We are now staffing things out in preparation for a good dialogue. That means preparing pieces of paper setting forth in detail what we already know. Symes Jones has also written the first draft of the piece of paper that is to go to the White House. Symes is not exactly a genius. But he has an excellent instinct for what the management wants. The draft will naturally reflect Campbell's present views. The paper could, of course, be redrafted at the meeting or afterward, but, unfortunately, it will also incorporate the facts that support Campbell's conclusions. Those will be hard to change. And Campbell would naturally ask Symes to do the redrafting. That would make it possible to hold changes to a minimum. So the draft is an excellent guide to what the meeting will decide."

"Why didn't you write it?" asked the Ambassador.

"I offered, but Campbell said, in his reasonable way, that I was too much of a partisan. So let Symes do it. He is a partisan, but he is Campbell's partisan without ever saying so which means he is nonpartisan. I agreed quite cheerfully because it was Campbell's privilege to decide anyway."

"We will have to get the meeting to reject the whole draft. Start fresh."

"That won't be easy. Most of the people will be there not because they are interested or informed but to protect the interest of their agency in the issue. They will go along with Campbell for they depend on his goodwill to keep them in."

"There will be some others?"

"Yes, but mostly people Campbell has invited because he knows where they stand."

"Well, we will simply have to persuade them that Campbell is wrong."

"That will be hard too, for Campbell will define the issue so that he may, in fact, be right."

"The position of Dr. Campbell seems to be pretty strong," said the Ambassador. "But shouldn't we give it a try?"

"Oh sure," said O'Donnell. "By all means."

.

The meeting assembled in Worth Campbell's office at 3 P.M. Earlier there is too much danger of interruption by late-comers hurriedly and apologetically making their entrance after an unduly prolonged lunch. Symes Jones's copies were available for distribution. Each was marked *Secret* and *Draft* and was numbered in ink in Symes's handwriting. Each recipient was requested to return his copy at the end of the meeting. These were a trifle more than normal precautions. But it was Worth Campbell's practice to take White House business with the utmost seriousness, and this also explained why copies had not been circulated in advance. This last also eliminated the danger that the recipients would come in with a great many unnecessary amendments.

A meeting such as this, Worth Campbell had years ago learned, cannot be small. Too many agencies have a legitimate concern, and, in any case, Campbell wanted to be sure everyone had a fair hearing. That was what the White House wanted. So when everyone was present, the big room was more than comfortably full. Three men shared the leather sofa, their knees rising awkwardly to the level of their chins. Three more were in the big leather armchairs to which Worth Campbell always moved from his desk for informal conversations with a visiting envoy. These six were either amateurs or men with little real interest in the proceedings. However admirable for easy talk, no man can address a meeting with authority from the depths of a sofa or armchair. The determined or articulate men had chosen the plain leather chairs or the even more Spartan metal ones that lined the walls. They put their briefcases on the floor between the chair legs; to relax, they tipped back against the walls. When their eyes wandered from the speaker, they looked at the framed and autographed photos on the wall behind Worth Campbell's chair — Lucius Clay, John J. McCloy, John Foster Dulles, Allen Welsh Dulles, Paul Hoffman, Averell Harriman, Clare Boothe Luce, Herbert Hoover, Jr., Nathan Pusey, several more who could not be so readily identified. The meeting could have been moved to a conference room, but Worth Campbell was more at home in his office and more immediately accessible by telephone in case of emergency. He also had a somewhat greater feeling of command. Present were one civilian and three officers, all in civilian clothes, from the office of the Assistant Secretary of Defense (International Affairs), including the Deputy Assistant Secretary (Far East and Latin American Affairs) and the Regional Director (Western Hemisphere). The Special Assistant for Counter Insurgency and Special Activities was also there from the Joint Staff of the Joint Chiefs of Staff together with two deputies. Two men were present from CIA and two from USIA. Two had come from AID including Dr. Richard Williams Kent. Dr. Kent had some difficulty in concealing his eagerness and also his nervousness. He swallowed frequently. It was the first meeting of such importance to which he had ever been invited. A Deputy Assistant Secretary of State for Educational and Cultural Affairs had been asked because Dr. Kent had been asked. This was to maintain parity. Were education in Puerto Santos to come up, someone from that shop would have a legitimate claim to be heard. Two men were present from the office of the Assistant Secretary of State for Intelligence and Research and two from the office of the Assistant Secretary of State for Economic Affairs. The scruffy-looking man in the tweed jacket from Policy Planning was there along with an assistant. His dandruff seemed worse. Pethwick was present. So in addition to Symes Jones were Bill O'Donnell and two younger men from O'Donnell's office including the well-tailored youngster whose name gave Worth Campbell trouble. The head of the Sugar Policy Staff of the Agricultural Stabilization and Conservation Service of the Department of Agriculture was there and also the Director of the American Republics Division of the Department of Commerce. The Treasury was to have been represented by the Director, Office of Developing Nations, but he did not show up. Alone among the departments of government, the Treasury cannot be counted upon to cover all meetings of importance. At the beginning of the meeting, the Ambassador to the Organization of American States was also missing.

He came in five minutes late, very apologetic and even more so when everyone including those deep in the couches stood up until a seat was found for him.

One of the girls in the Assistant Secretary's office was present by the corner of his desk with a pad to take notes. The Assistant Secretary opened the meeting by thanking everyone present and briefly explaining its purpose. He stressed especially his desire for a free, frank dialogue with — as he smilingly said — "no holds barred." No policy was sacred; certainly none could be so regarded when the White House asked for review. Nothing was off limits for the dialogue. He would say a brief word on the present policy. It was not a rigid policy; it was one of keeping a close eye on developments, one, in a word, of watchful waiting. We wanted to minimize the risk of Communism, we tried to be sure that we did business with governments that had, in a sense, proved themselves. No one, he supposed, and certainly not the President, wanted our aid and diplomatic support to be used to build a Communist regime. There would be agreement on this; he would not say more for he did not want to seem to be prejudging the issue. He asked for a general dialogue. It got off to a slow start. Nearly everyone, however, was impressed by Campbell's open-mindedness.

·

In concerting their strategy the evening before, Bill O'Donnell and the Ambassador to the OAS had decided that the latter should lead off. People associated with diplomacy have a tendency to defer to age and rank, especially rank. Also O'Donnell was not a persuasive man. His choice of language regularly confirmed his opposition in the rightness and even the righteousness of its views. It was also understood that they would hold their fire. Both were experienced men and knew that all meetings in the Department of State open on a highly undirected note. No serious argument can usefully be offered until this period has passed.

Things went reasonably to form. After a few moments' silence with everyone looking a little uneasily at everyone else, the untidy man from Policy Planning asked if it would not be useful at the outset to define the American and free world interest in Puerto Santos. When no one responded, he took this as agreement and proceeded. Everyone recognized the irrelevance of his remarks but pretended, nonetheless, to listen closely. It appeared, generally, that Puerto Santos was not of primary and not of secondary but because of its proximity to the Canal was of more than tertiary interest to free world security. Under no circumstance should the Communists be allowed to cross the Rostow truce line at this point. He went on to urge that we be prepared at all times to rethink our policy and to regear our planning and reorient our programs accordingly. His colleague from Policy Planning looked uncomfortable. It was speeches like this that gave the organization a bad name. Before the speaker had begun to show any perceptible loss of power, the Assistant Secretary's secretary came in with a note. Peering through his glasses, Campbell selected from a choice of buttons on the console and picked up the telephone. A hush fell over the room.

The conversation which none could hear was very brief, but quite a few noticed that the Assistant Secretary's manner was even firmer and more decisive over the telephone than in the meeting. He was a man, obviously, with reserves of strength. It was an emergency call from Mrs. Campbell. Their boy had been picked up for speeding in Falls Church, and the police officer had promised to give him a hard time. The man from Policy Planning resumed but with visibly less authority. During the interruption his colleague had slipped him a note saying, "It might be good strategy to cut it a little short — if you agree." A few observations on general nuclear strategy, a reference to the parallels between the present position of Communism and that of the Confederacy after Fort Sumter and a plea that everyone be guided "by the numbers in this situation," and he was finished.

Soon the meeting was well under way. A lean, healthy-looking man from the Joint Staff sketched in succinct terms the present thinking on military action to prevent a Communist take-over. The Air Force had agreed to a plan for bombing communications with Flores, and it was now before the Chiefs. It contained an important change in thinking. Reflecting the present assessment of the Communist threat, bombing was now designed not to keep the Communists out of the capital city but to keep them in. It would need to be combined, they recognized, with maximum emphasis on winning the hearts and minds of the people. Accordingly, the closest liaison would be maintained with the Agency for International Development (AID) and the U.S. Information Agency. The men from the latter agencies bowed in general acknowledgment of their need.

The Sugar Policy man from the Department of Agriculture then said that, given the present attitudes on the Hill toward the Miró Administration, it would be tough to keep the present sugar quota. He implied, without quite saying so, that Miró would do well to get himself an experienced Washington lawyer and learn a few things from Martínez about how things were done in this town. "You don't get sugar quotas up there outa love." Interest sharpened. Here was the world of political legerdemain which most of those present knew only from reading Drew Pearson and about Senator Thomas J. Dodd. Also, the man from Agriculture depended not so much on words as on a succession of confidential winks, meaningful twistings of the mouth, and thumbs and fingers made into a circle and punched knowingly with an index finger. This required close attention. The Ambassador, studying the man's age and accent, allowed himself to imagine he had come in with Huey Long. Worth Campbell thanked the sugar man when he showed signs of launching an unduly lengthy eulogy of Senator Allen J. Ellender. He suggested that perhaps they should get even closer to the subject. He asked the senior CIA man for their current estimate of Communist infiltration in the government of Puerto Santos and the resulting threat to the free world.

This was slightly dangerous. The Agency was not as alarmed as the Assistant Secretary would have wished.

Their younger men were showing the same uncertainty of mission that was to be found in so many other places. And their man in Puerto Santos was clearly under the influence of Joe Hurd. But early in such a meeting one must have the intelligence position. Bypassing it would be noticed. And as it developed Campbell's worries were groundless. The gist of the Agency position was that the situation was unclear. They did not estimate an early Communist take-over, but when pressed a little by Campbell, their man, after a whispered consultation with his colleague, said that it could not be excluded. He summarized by saying that the Agency regarded the situation as unclear. He asked all to keep in mind that these matters were highly classified.

The Ambassador to the OAS judged that the time had come to intervene.

"These people had thirty years of the dictatorship of Martínez. Now they seem to have a good and decent government. I have known some of these people, either personally or their families, and I think they want to be friends of ours. I say we should recognize this government and give it some help — the kind of help we gave to Martínez. Mr. O'Donnell here, who has followed things closely, agrees with me. The President is leaning that way which is why we are having this meeting. I've read the cables, and there seems to be full agreement" — here the Ambassador paused for emphasis and repeated himself — "there is full agreement among our people on the spot on supporting the Miró Administration. People who do things usually get called Communists. That is something they probably learned from us, so it's no objection. If we don't support Miró, we will get something worse."

It was a very effective speech. The Ambassador knew how to hit the right note of authority. For just a moment even Campbell felt a twinge of uneasiness. Could the meeting be swung around so that it did something foolish? He saw with more alarm that Pethwick was moving in.

Campbell gave the floor to Pethwick and then held him off for a word first. He said he hoped the Ambassador did not suggest that anyone was making any loose charges about Communism. They would all agree on not countenancing that sort of thing. But they would also have to agree that Communists did exist and were active. They were a danger just as McCarthyism was a danger. Their task was to avoid the one without resorting to the other. He might make one other point. They had before them the old problem of giving proper weight but not excessive weight to the views of those on the ground. There was the matter of perspective. There was also the old disease of clientitis — the tendency to see things through the eyes of the government to which you were accredited. He supposed that he had suffered from that himself, that he had sometimes pulled an oar for Adenauer and Jean Monnet. And unanimity of view down there could be discounted a little bit; they all worked closely together, and in fact all of their recommendations had come in at the same time yesterday couched in almost exactly the same language. One guessed that they had been pretty well discussed — which was as it should be. But their views should be weighed. He didn't go so far as Winston

Churchill who once said that the British Empire was built on two principles: "Never trust the man on the spot; never yield to anything but force." It was another of Campbell's rare resorts to the lighter touch. There was an appreciative titter which promptly stopped as Pethwick got under way.

Pethwick was still angry at what the Ambassador had said. It took him some time to say what he had to say for he repeated himself with some frequency. But the gist was not complex. Martínez had given that country thirty years of stable government, and from being there he knew the people had been happy. (Pethwick had evidently not been impressed by Churchill.) As for Miró he could only say that "Miró was . . . was a dog!"

Pethwick was not persuasive. However, he was helped by O'Donnell. O'Donnell said Pethwick's views on Miró like those on Martínez's popular support were not to be trusted. In proof he recalled the telegrams predicting Martínez's survival and implied, not too obliquely, that Pethwick had brown-nosed the dictator to the point of acute sinus. All this was true. But its vigor diverted attention from the case that the old Ambassador had made. And it violated a cardinal rule of American diplomacy which is that one never dwells in public on the mistakes of another man. This is a sensible rule. Mistakes are inevitable. If they are not allowed to others, they will not be allowed to you. So reciprocity is essential. At this juncture one of the men from the Office of the Assistant Secretary of Defense (International Affairs) broke in to say "purely for the record" that the Air Force plans on bombing and counter-insurgency action had not been approved by the Office of the Secretary of Defense. One of his assistants, an Army colonel, then volunteered his purely personal opinion that they might not be as effective as the Air Force expected.

The military were questioned knowledgeably on the point by several civilians, and then the discussion returned to the sugar quotas and to land reform. Campbell's stenographer walked over to the door and turned on the lights. A vicious winter rain was beating on the windows above and behind the leather couch. Campbell listened impassively, patiently.

In the course of every meeting, Worth Campbell knew, there comes a time when impatience and even boredom induce tractability. Decisions that might earlier be deplored will now be accepted by men who are tired, have engagements, want to pee, or are incipient alcoholics. That time would come soon. Presently he suggested that it was time "to redefine the issue." To what extent, he asked, could we exclude the danger of a Communist takeover if we gave Miró all-out backing. The Ambassador and Bill O'Donnell both protested that this was not the issue. The issue was whether Miró was a reasonable risk. Campbell asked, with almost deliberate gentleness, if, where Communism was concerned, it wasn't a good principle to try to minimize risk. He would welcome an indication of dissent. Heads nodded in general approval. Campbell then asked if this could be taken as agreement, in principle, that they should continue the present policy of watchful waiting. He would welcome a preliminary indication of feeling. Who disagreed? People looked rather uneasily at the Ambassador and Bill O'Donnell who, with the man from the Sugar Policy Staff, were the only ones immediately to indicate opposition. All held up their hands. However, after a moment they were joined by one of Bill O'Donnell's boys, a man from the Bureau of Intelligence and Research, and, more ambiguously, by one of the men from CIA. He put up his hand and then, after a glance around the room and at his colleague, took it down again. There was a more stalwart dissenting vote from one of the officers from the office of the Assistant Secretary of Defense. Captain González's initiative had not been entirely without effect. The man from Agriculture insisted on explaining his vote. Watchful waiting was a policy of inaction; he was, he said, by nature a man of action. The Ambassador asked Campbell to put the question affirmatively: How many thought it would be wise to support the Miró Administration now that we had six months' experience with it? Campbell said he thought everyone would perhaps agree that there had been a fairly full and free chance for expression of opinion ending with a vote on the policy as presently defined. He ignored a request from O'Donnell that he ask how many had no position, and several present looked at O'Donnell with mild hostility. Campbell then said he did not wish to rush matters, but perhaps they should get down to work on the piece of paper. There are many kinds of managed democracy.

Numerous suggestions were now forthcoming on how to clarify the language, sharpen the dialogue, be more constructive, emphasize the essential point, avoid being "quite so categorical on matters where we cannot be entirely sure" and on how "to leave ourselves a little avenue of escape without hedging the point unduly." The man from Commerce asked for insertion of a sentence stressing the importance of "a free flow of private trade and capital regardless of what government we might be backing." The Assistant Secretary listened attentively to all these suggestions and asked Symes Jones to see that they were fully considered. The Ambassador to OAS asked if it could be made clear that the decision against supporting Miró — as he took it to be — was not unanimous. Worth Campbell replied: "Of course, sir. There is no coercion here." From time to time a man excused himself and looking at his watch or frowning hurried away. Presently the meeting came to an end.

The Ambassador and O'Donnell were unhappy but not surprised. Dr. Richard Williams Kent was merely unhappy. He hadn't enjoyed the meeting for, in spite of himself, he had kept going over his speech about Roberto Ryan. And he hadn't been asked to say a word. At dinner that evening even his wife noticed that he seemed depressed.

17

ONCE THE BASIC DECISION had been reached to recommend that the policy of watchful waiting be continued on an interim basis, Worth Campbell moved fairly promptly to communicate it to the President. Symes Jones, as noted, took charge of preparation of the final draft of the piece of paper. This was then circulated to the offices of those principally concerned including all who had attended the meeting. Along with it went a reminder that suggestions "should, of course, be within the general framework of policy as hitherto agreed." These were incorporated as applicable, initials were then obtained, the final draft was approved at a meeting with the Secretary, and within ten days the piece of paper was on the way to the White House. This was two days before Christmas.

Before then, inevitably, there had been newspaper leaks and even an occasional small headline. "U.S. TO KEEP FREEZE ON RED REGIME." "NO CHANGE ON PUERTO SANTOS." "COMMUNISTS IN MIRO GOVERNMENT A BAR TO AID." This was highly premature, and Worth Campbell had William

Henry McWilliams, Jr., deny one day at the regular press briefing that a decision had been reached. "Our Puerto Santos policy is naturally under continuous review," McWilliams said, reading from a typewritten sheet of paper, "and nothing will be decided until the President has reached a decision." None of this was of great interest in the United States. Newswise, as the more uncouth members of the press put it, Puerto Santos was on the back burner. But it was news in Flores. In the Martínez years the headlines of the two decipherable papers in the capital were often dictated by the old *Jefe* himself and were sometimes identical and always idiosyncratic. Once they reported over eight columns an excellent medical finding on the President including a reassuring reduction in albumen, sugar and blood pressure, and a negative Wassermann. After six months of press freedom, the art of assessing events was still imperfectly developed. But no editor thought these rumors from Washington unimportant. The resulting news stories impressed both Miró and those who did not wish him well.

The President in Washington might have been annoyed at this premature publicity. It limited his freedom of decision, for now a judgment in favor of Miró would be known to have reversed one by his experts, and it would be known that it deliberately discounted a Communist danger. This any President dislikes — if the Reds one day took over, many would remember the disregard of professional advice. Fortunately in this instance the annoyance was well-controlled. A veteran of many years in Washington, the President knew that such leaks affecting his decisions were part of the game. Unlike more impatient predecessors, he was of philosophical mood. When it came to the White House he read Worth Campbell's report with attention and with no evident irritation at its comparative absence of surprise.

MEMORANDUM FOR THE PRESIDENT

Pursuant to request to the Assistant Secretary of State for Inter-American Affairs and U.S. Coordinator, Alliance for Progress, we have pleasure in submitting herewith. . . .

It is regretted that this has taken some time. It will be appreciated that a thoroughgoing review. . . .

It is to be expected that on so complex a matter as our policy toward Puerto Santos and the provisional Administration which seized power following the fall of President Luis Miguel Martínez-Obregón there would be differences of opinion. It is, however, the considered and predominant view of those concerned, and of the agencies they represent, that to at this time extend recognition and economic and military aid to the revolutionary administration would be to invite unacceptable risks to U.S. hemisphere and free world security. . . .

The presence in one or more key posts of the Miró Administration of known or suspected members of the Communist Party. . . .

. . . aware that it is not an ideal solution we nonetheless recommend continuation of the present policy of watchful waiting.

. . . when Miró Administration has proved that it is willing to dispose with potentially unfriendly elements we would not rule out prompt review. . . .

It is stressed that if any further information is needed we stand ready to promptly. . . .

The President noticed the reference to the "considered and predominant view" and was not entirely reassured. The considered and predominant view had been in error before. There was the considered and predominant view that invasion would succeed at the Bay of Pigs. And that a small force of Americans would quickly pacify Vietnam. And that Juan Bosch was a menace to the free world. He would perhaps have been more concerned had he known just how this particular consensus had been established. But the reference to the predominant view had another implication. It warned that he would face a phalanx of experts and officials if he decided to get into the matter. And he would need to probe very deeply indeed, for otherwise he would seem to be reversing the massed wisdom of the government in a somewhat arbitrary fashion. Meanwhile there was Israel, Egypt and Syria; and a new African crisis; and the burgeoning population and dwindling food supplies of India; and the mystery of what was happening in China; and the unfortunate clarity of what was occurring in Indo-China; and the Budget; and the State of the Union Message; and the chronically poor condition of the National Committee. Time could not easily be spared for Puerto Santos. On specific matters, Grant Worthing Campbell is a man of formidable power. But, to repeat, it would be a great injustice to suppose that he ever looks at things in this way.

·

A short statement was authorized saying that no change in the Puerto Santos policy was presently contemplated. This, too, was large — and devastating — news in Flores.

·

Worth Campbell had not again seen Andrés Medina Alvarez. The old man had been making the rounds of AID, the International Bank, the International Development Association, the Ex-Im Bank, the Inter-American Development Bank and the Department of Agriculture. Everywhere he had been greeted with courtesy. Everywhere he was told or allowed to sense what he already knew: "Until the State Department comes round, I am afraid there isn't much we can do." When the Ambassador and Bill O'Donnell told him about the meeting in Worth Campbell's office and what it probably meant, he decided to go home. A few days before Christmas he said good-bye to the Ambassador with regret and to the Puerto Santos Representative with real pleasure and took the shuttle to New York. There he visited for a day or two with a friend who now headed the New York office of one of the Canadian chartered banks and then went out to Kennedy to catch the Pan Am flight back home. Despite the fact that he was still traveling tourist, he was ushered into the Clipper Club. He did not recognize nor did anyone point out to him a fellow passenger on the same flight, also waiting in the Club. It was Juan César Martínez.

·

When the term ended, young Martínez had bid an unemotional farewell to the University of Michigan and an only slightly more touching good-bye to the good-natured girl with the ample breasts. In New York he had visited an uncle, a year or two his father's senior, who had vegetated there for many years as deputy head of the delegation to the United Nations. He lived on in a cavernous apartment in the Waldorf Towers and seemed well supplied with money. He had aged. The pouches under his eyes, a family trademark, were more pendulous than ever. He was also very fat and walked with difficulty. He introduced Juan with repugnance to a blond woman of mature years and extreme vulgarity as "your aunt" and looked pleased when she bade them enjoy "a nice talk" and left. They lunched together on large steaks, a little cold and tasting of charcoal, sent up from the hotel kitchen. The old man complimented his nephew on his decision to return to Puerto Santos. "Someone wrote to ask me if I would tell you to come back. I didn't do it. I no longer pay attention to such matters. I expect they will be glad to have a Martinez running things again."

"They have told me I should stay out of politics."

"That is what I always used to tell your father. Run the country and stay out of politics." The theme caught the older man's fancy, and he enlarged on it at some length. Finally he came back to business. "You should make me delegate to the Children's Fund. I do not wish to listen to those long speeches in the Assembly any more, and I am very fond of children."

"I wouldn't count on it, Uncle. Times change. My father's kind of government belongs to the past. Anyway, I don't suppose you need to work."

"You are right to keep up with the times, my boy. That is something I always advised your father to do. If he had taken my advice, he would still be in office. I read in the paper they are making your Uncle Jaime drive a garbage truck. That is stupid. He will get drunk and kill someone. If you are going to keep up with the times, hire a good man to handle your statistics. You must have a large annual increase in your national income. The Americans now demand it; I learned this in the Economic and Social Council. Will you perhaps see your mother?"

"Yes. My journey is really to visit her."

At the airport Juan Martínez noticed the dark-clad, dignified, rather handsome old man and guessed he might be someone of importance. But he had no idea who he was.

Christmas Carol: Feliz Año

THE CUSTOM in the Puerto Santos army runs to liberal Christmas leaves extending to Three Kings' Day. The generals were especially generous this year. While officers and men of detachments that were thought loyal to Miró and the Provisional Government (or disloyal to the old generals) were on holiday, a battalion that had been held back for the purpose drove to the palace and arrested Miró and half a dozen members of the cabinet. They were holding a meeting on the financial situation. Miró was charged with tolerating Communism, encouraging subversive propaganda and failing to solve the economic problems of the nation, and the same day put aboard a plane bound for Miami. The generals had taken note of the warnings that Washington might not be friendly to the idea of a military government. They were determined to please, and they had reflected on the decades of good relations between Flores and Washington under the previous regime. The query from the former ambassador that had followed his restaurant encounter

with Assistant Secretary Grant Worthing Campbell had
been to one of the generals. It had been taken, naturally
enough, to be a clue to State Department thinking. The
generals sent out to the small ranch some twenty or thirty
kilometers from Flores where the wife of the old dictator
had lived in semi-seclusion for many years and asked
Juan César Martínez, who was visiting there, to come
into the palace. He came readily enough, although it is
not clear that he had much choice. General Pérez, speaking for his colleagues, asked him to become Provisional President and head a cabinet that would consist
of both military men and civilians. They told him this
would be in keeping with the great destiny of his family.
They let it be known that his duties would not be onerous.
All of the decisions and most of the administration would
be in the hands of the good friends and loyal collabora-
tors who were with him now. He would have time, as a
young man, to enjoy himself. They had been forced to
assume power in order to save their country from the imminent threat of Communism, socialism, atheism and in-
solvency — the latter, although they didn't say so, being
most poignantly their own. All this, omitting only the last,
they had already announced. They would carry forward their great task of national rejuvenation in his name
and on his behalf. This, too, they would now take the liberty of announcing. Washington had already indicated,
through various channels, that it would be favorable. The
Martínez name would electrify the country. They did not
feel that he had any choice but to accept.

·

Washington responded well. The more emotional liberals in the Senate and House were at home. Their protests were aired only in such distant vehicles as the Salem *News* and the Fort Smith *Times Record,* and *Newsday.* The *New York Times,* Washington *Post* and Louisville *Courier-Journal* expressed regret to an audience which was, on the whole, still suffering from a surfeit of Christmas food, drink and unnaturally manifested goodwill. The Ambassador to the OAS, Bill O'Donnell, the young men in the White House were sorry. But to none of them was it a surprise. For since the meeting in Worth Campbell's office had adjourned, they had assumed that it was only a matter of time.

Assistant Secretary Campbell, though he had not predicted the change or counted on it coming so soon, was undeniably relieved. The threat of Communism in Puerto Santos had now been extirpated. He could look forward for the rest of his tour of duty in Washington to a stable and friendly government in Flores. And the free world would have a friend there for many years thereafter. It was, as he said to Symes Jones, one country off his platter.

Not quite, for as any strategist of his experience knew, it was always necessary to move quickly to consolidate a victory. Once the Communists and the fellow travelers and their stooges saw what had happened to them they would rally their forces. Though Miró, Madera and Ryan were no longer in a position to be a threat, others, one had to assume, were always waiting to move in. And they would be the same men trained in the same hard school of conspiracy and violent action. Before the old year was out, Worth Campbell had got approval, in principle, for restoring full diplomatic relations with the new government. Announcement need only wait until the papers were reasonably involved with some other event so as to minimize irresponsible criticism by those who had committed themselves emotionally to Miró, Madera and Ryan. One had always to reckon with the reactions of the impractical amateur, but fortunately they were predictable. Meanwhile, the new Martínez Administration was given private assurances. Recognition came on the fourth of January in the middle of an unprecedented blizzard in Nebraska, and Ambassador and Mrs. Pethwick, still according to accepted international practice accredited to the government of Puerto Santos, took the Pan Am flight for Flores the following day. After many months in a borrowed house, Mrs. Pethwick looked forward to being once more with the things she loved. In addition to his wife, and in all respects more interesting, Pethwick took with him a package. This consisted of an outright grant of twenty million dollars to help pay the bills of the new administration for, not unexpectedly after months of flirting with leftist schemes, it was very short of money. Things were better but not a great deal better than when Miró and Medina took over. Now there would be enough to underwrite the payroll of the Army and the public officials for several months — what Campbell called a good long breathing spell. Pethwick also took with him a promise that the rest of the AID program would be promptly reinstituted. There would be a new Experimental Farm to replace the one that had been divided up. A new team would study land reform. He brought informal assurance that the sugar quota would definitely be continued and a little something added from what had once belonged to Cuba. Last but not least — military aid was restored. This would emphasize, appropriately, riot control and counter-insurgency hardware. Since it was important to nip any counter-revolution in the bud, Pethwick was authorized to say that the year's program would be airlifted in a single flight of C-130's just as soon as Martínez had assented to its need. Pethwick was instructed to urge upon Martínez the importance of an eventual promise of free elections.

．

Pethwick felt a spasm of nostalgia as he made his way to the marble palace but, a cold and wholly professional diplomat, he dismissed it for the moment as the beginning of a slight attack of dysentery. But then he felt it again when he was shown into the presence of the young President. He had the same short, swarthy, slightly stocky, wholly undistinguished appearance as his father. He had the same heavy cheeks and receding forehead, the same intelligent, bright, untrustworthy eyes. He made Pethwick feel very much at home. He spoke with pleasure of his years in the United States. He told Pethwick that his would not be a passive administration. He would draw at all points on American experience and precedent. He would use the knowledge that he had acquired in his university studies and extra-curricular discussions in the United States. Pethwick reported home at length and with warm approval. His only complaint, indeed, was that his automobile had not yet been fixed.

.

Young Martínez was as good as his word. He personally met the planes bringing in the arms. In accordance with the prudent practice in that part of the world, he had them taken to the basement of the palace. There he personally superintended their distribution to a group of younger officers and their men with whom he had made contact in previous days. Their sudden appearance with new and impressive American firepower brought over to their side the detachments that General Pérez had sent home for the holidays. While many had appreciated the vacation, some had been a little angered by the transparent character of the General's tactics. In all of this, as he told Pethwick, Juan Martínez was drawing heavily on a seminar of Professor Schmiltz. "The key to power is a monopoly of ultimate force." In Puerto Santos, obviously, that was the army.

Possessed of a monopoly of ultimate force, Martínez proceeded to reorganize his cabinet. He sent General Pérez as Consul General to Miami. As he told the General and later Pethwick, he was inspired in making this appointment not so much by General Pérez's qualifications, including his quite intelligible English, as by the fact that this same post had been selected by the United States for General Wessin y Wessin when it had seemed desirable to remove him from the Dominican Republic. Other senior generals were dispatched to London, Madrid, Rome, Buenos Aires and New Orleans. He recalled confidentially to Pethwick that Professor Schmiltz had once said that "conspirators dispersed cannot conspire." He remembered also that President John F. Kennedy, whom he professed greatly to admire, had sent an admiral who promised to make difficulty as Ambassador Extraordinary and Plenipotentiary to Lisbon.

So rapidly and peacefully had the Miró Administration been brought to an end that the fire brigade of Washington newspapermen had never been dispatched. Additionally, it had been Christmas, and the real news in Latin America as elsewhere is in the Communist take-overs. There is much less interest in the much more common *golpe* by generals designed to stop Communism in its tracks. Young Martínez and his Michigan background justified a journey by only a few reporters and feature writers who sought to tell something of his personality, economic plans, methods of government and, hopefully, of his sex life. They reported back that his would not be a passive administration, that he was drawing heavily on American precedent and the knowledge that he had acquired while studying in the United States. They added that, in the Martínez tradition, he was busy consolidating power. In those early days Martínez made a point of being available to the press.

·

Later, Juan Martínez showed himself even less passive. Along in January he announced that Puerto Santos would have a Five Year Plan. Its inspiration was not the Soviet plans but those that Harvard University through its famous Development Advisory Service had drawn up for Pakistan, Iran and Colombia. He said he would welcome American suggestions. Talking with Pethwick and later with reporters, he recalled that the Institute which Dr. Worthing Campbell had headed in his university days had cooperated with the Harvard people. His sympathy could be assured. Dr. Campbell himself, he noted perhaps unnecessarily, was now the head of the Alliance for Progress.

Later in the same week he took two even more dramatic steps. First he deeded all of the Martínez properties — the sugar *centrales,* coffee *fincas,* cattle ranches, urban real estate, oil company, bauxite concession, cement mill, power company, business firms and import houses together with franchises for American cigarettes, Coca-Cola, automobiles, pharmaceuticals, electrical goods and the Latin American edition of *Time* — to the people of Puerto Santos.

It is doubtful if socialism ever came so quickly, so completely, so undramatically and with so little complaint from owners of property as in Puerto Santos. Martínez owned the property. The deed of gift was executed in a minute or two. The revolution was over with the stroke of a pen. For once its power far exceeded that of any sword.

The land reform later in the same week was only slightly more controversial. Martínez owned most of the good land including a good deal of the urban property. There were really very few landlords of importance left to complain. Those who had survived were paid the full value of their land as it had been assessed for taxes and compensated with three percent non-negotiable bonds maturing in fifty years.

Washington, however, was interested, and Pethwick was instructed by Worth Campbell to inquire, if cautiously, as to the young dictator's intentions. The interview took some time. Martínez pointed out that he had learned in the United States that the highest obligation of the more fortunate is to the society of which they are members. He had heard this principle enunciated at a University Commencement by a speaker whose name he could not recall, by Mr. Henry Ford II and, as he recalled, in a television interview by former President Dwight D. Eisenhower. He felt deeply his responsibility to these distinguished American teachers to carry it into practical effect. Also it was surely wrong to confuse the socialization of land and industry with the gift of one's property to one's country. He thought that Ambassador Pethwick would be judged wrong, even by lawyers in the United States, in suggesting that nationalizing one's own property was banned by the Hickenlooper Amendment. "Would Senator Hickenlooper, who had once spoken at Michigan, wish to prevent Governor Nelson Rockefeller from presenting the very large Rockefeller holdings to the State of New York? Would he have prevented President Kennedy, had the latter wished, from giving the Merchandise Mart in Chicago to the United States government?" When Pethwick, rising to the occasion, said that people might consider a situation where a government held all the private property to be Communism, Juan Martínez explained that Communism was a much different, a much more highly developed state of society than socialism. Communism could come only after all trace of past pecuniary and bourgeois attitudes had been erased. Only amateurs confused the two; this had been greatly emphasized at Michigan in a course he had taken on Comparative Economic Systems. He assured Pethwick that Puerto Santos was by no stretch of the imagination ready for Communism. In reporting back, Pethwick emphasized the latter point which was the one he had most fully grasped.

On the land reform, young Martínez was equally reassuring. "This was recommended, Mr. Ambassador, by all six studies made by the University of Wisconsin during the days of my father. They all urged prompt and vigorous implementation as I can show you. And this my father repeatedly promised. I am only keeping his promise. You thought well of him, everybody tells me. As to paying off the landowners with bonds that cannot be sold, that idea I have taken over in the most precise detail, except for our slightly higher interest rate, from the plan followed by General of the Army Douglas MacArthur in the land reform which he put into effect by his personal decree in Japan and Korea on behalf of the occupying powers. I once wrote a seminar paper on that plan. It is true that these bonds may in time be rendered more or less valueless by inflation, and they will have to be held by the owner nonetheless. But that, as I learned from my study in Michigan, happened also in Japan and Korea

and there very quickly. It was my thought to call our reform The MacArthur Plan."

The name almost caught on, and so it came about that
Martínez was praised on the floor of the House of Representatives in Washington by two elderly Republicans for
following in the footprints of the great American captain
and denounced by a third for taking his name in vain.

Pethwick made a further call when Martínez recognized the Soviet Union, Czechoslovakia, Poland, Ru-
mania, Cuba, China and Hungary. However, he was
somewhat reassured when Martínez said that except in the
case of Cuba and China it was to support Washington's
policy of building bridges to Eastern Europe. As regards
the other two he quoted both Professor Schmiltz and the
American Secretary of State to the effect that, in the
American practice, diplomatic recognition of a government implied no approval of that regime. He sought to
follow American practice.

Pethwick called again when Martínez announced that
the palm tree schools would be taken over by a new organization built along the lines of a political party which
would have responsibility both for popular and political
education and these would be compulsory for the young.
Compulsory education, Martínez reminded Pethwick, was
an old American idea, and while in the United States he
had heard many people emphasize the importance of education in citizenship for young and old. It was a proper
function for a political party. Once, while in Michigan, he
had attended a political discussion group organized for
just such purposes by Mr. Neil Staebler, the State Chair-

man of the Democratic Party. Mr. Staebler lived in Ann Arbor. He planned, he told Pethwick, to call the whole development the December 25 Movement, in spite of the fact that the revolution had taken place two days later. It would emphasize to Washington the spirit in which he acted; Christmas meant much to North Americans. Pethwick was again, although not totally, reassured.

But Washington was not reassured. And in February when Martínez retired all of the older officers of the army, announced that it would henceforth be called a militia and placed one of his most energetic supporters, a political activist named Aragón, at its head, Pethwick was told to make Washington's disapproval known in the strongest terms. Martínez explained to Pethwick that in reforming the military he was really bent on conserving his resources for the most important things. It had been axiomatic at Michigan in the courses in economic development that armies were an unnecessary drain on the resources of a poor country. But this was not accepted. Nor was his statement that the reform was modeled on the National Guard. Nor was his suggestion that he had selected Aragón because, as in the case of the Pentagon, there was need for strong civilian control. Pethwick was asked home for consultation. Mrs. Pethwick had once more to leave behind the things she loved.

·

The Director General of the Foreign Service had again dropped in on the Deputy Under Secretary for Administration.

"I hear Pethwick goes to Ireland."

"That's right."

"He blotted his copybook a bit this second round in Flores. Not seeing what that young Martínez was up to."

"I think Ireland is all right. Good enough so we don't admit to his making a mistake, not big enough to be a big kick upstairs. We couldn't send him to France or Spain or Portugal or Formosa."

"No, not any of those. I still think he might have been better teaching in a university. Do you suppose when De Valera dies, Pethwick will try to go too?"

"Don't joke about these matters. How do you think Worth will be as Under Secretary?"

.

How Worth Campbell will be as Under Secretary is for the future to decide. He is certainly not unhappy about the promotion. In the war against the international Communist conspiracy there are bound, as in all wars, to be setbacks. It is important that, in face of such setbacks, the free nations close ranks and that free governments do likewise. He cannot be sorry that he benefited from such a closing of ranks. And while Worth Campbell regrets as much as any man the developments in Flores, they are also proof that he, and not the young men of uncertain mission, has the correct view of the Communist menace. It has been shown to exist.

Bill O'Donnell is not unhappy, although he may be if he does not see the need to close ranks.

The Ambassador to the OAS is not unhappy. He is philosophical. Unlike Bill O'Donnell, he has been right many times, and he knows how to behave.

Jose María Miró is not entirely unhappy. He is spending a year at the Economic Growth Center at Yale.

Joe Hurd is happy at least at the way his professional judgment of his own future has been validated. He has been selected out. During his enforced idleness in Washington, Pethwick, in accordance with custom, served on the selection board.

In a pleasant and not especially pretentious house in Estoril near Lisbon, Luis Miguel Martínez Obregón is not unhappy. He was never as clear as some others on the difference between capitalism, free enterprise, socialism and Communism. It is sufficient that his son seems to be showing the same sanguinary qualities that he himself displayed thirty years ago. He didn't know the boy had it in him. He liked especially the way he stuck it into old Pérez.

María is not unhappy. The new administration has given her a small pension on which she remains drunk.

Mrs. Pethwick is happy. In the lovely residence in Phoenix Park she will soon again be united with the things she loves. True, Pethwick must be approved by the Senate, but the Committee is headed by gentlemen.

Juan César Martínez is not unhappy although perhaps this is because he does not dwell on the future. He may have set in motion forces he cannot control. But he does not think so, and time alone will tell.

The people who got the land are very happy.

Luis Carlos Madera is probably not happy. Because of

his knowledge of the police dossiers and his outspoken tendencies it has been necessary to keep him in jail.

Whether Roberto Ryan is happy or unhappy cannot be told. He had been a Communist, like his father a distant but devoted follower of Leon Trotsky. Aragón had him shot.